DESERT CAPTIVE

Doc Beck Westerns Book 4

SARAH ELISABETH SAWYER

ROCKHAVEN PUBLISHING

PROLOGUE

The sun sagged in the western sky, signaling the end of the day. Tiny blossoms quivered in the fresh green grass of the hillside as Laramie Jones rode his horse Slate at a steady clip. Slate churned the greens and blues and pinks together beneath his pounding hooves.

Laramie leaned forward in the saddle as his horse labored up the steep hill. When he and the big gray were on a mission like this, they wouldn't stop until they saw it through to the end, even if night caught them out in the cold.

Laramie and Slate topped the ridge. The horse was quicker than him, angling to the right by instinct. Laramie looked that direction and saw, there, trotting down the other side of the hill, was the rogue steer they'd chased for half an hour. The steer was heading into the rocky country at the base of Wyoming's Medicine Bow Mountains.

Laramie let Slate lope after the steer, both of them feeling the urgency. Even the horse had sense enough to know the rocky foothills was no place for a critter at sunset. This fool steer didn't know Laramie was chasing after him for his own good, to steer him back before he ran himself off a cliff.

The steer vanished among the rocks at the base of the hill, a valley before the next hill started.

Reaching the base, Laramie guided the big gray onto a trail leading out of the green pastureland and into pure rocks. Fool, fool steer. Why didn't it know better than to run from good forage into the scraps of the world?

The scenario reminded Laramie of the prodigal son that Jesus told about in the Bible of a young man who abandoned all the comforts of home and ended up eating from pig troughs.

There were life lessons like that, everywhere a body looked, if they were paying attention.

Laramie pulled the big gray to a halt next to a wither's high boulder. He held his breath and listened. There was a crash to his left, followed by the braying of an animal in distress.

Slate's head turned that direction and Laramie eased off the reins to let the horse meander through the rocks. Laramie spotted the steer in a ravine ahead, legs folded beneath it, briars tangled in its horns. Looked like the steer slid into the ravine when trying to navigate the narrow ledge above.

Laramie swung down from the big gray, unhooking his lariat rope. He went to the edge of the ravine and the steer started thrashing with three of its legs. Laramie could see from the distance of thirty feet that the steer's right hind leg was broken.

Laramie sighed and returned to his gray, stroking the faithful horse on the neck. Slate was aging, same as him, but they were both still in the prime of life. Laramie was just passed his 40th birthday and the gray stood at half that age.

This wasn't their first failed mission, and they knew how to handle defeat. Still, it never got easy.

Laramie rehung his lariat and withdrew his Henry rifle from the scabbard. He paused, sighing deep. With a comforting squeeze of the gray's crest through his leather glove, Laramie went to the edge of the ravine and looked down at the steer. Its eyes were wild with rebellion.

"Sorry about this."

Laramie shouldered the rifle, took careful aim, and squeezed off a round. The pain-filled braying stopped.

This mission was over, but more work was waiting for Laramie and the big gray.

They were halfway back to the spring round-up camp, topping the third hill on the trip, when Laramie saw a lone figure cutting across the wide valley below, chaps flying as he rode hard.

It was Steve Bowers, one of Laramie's top hands.

As foreman of the McKinnon Ranch, Laramie Jones couldn't always go off chasing steers, but he was still a ranch hand, and he had good men like Steve to see that all ran right when he was absent.

But something bad had happened by the look on Steve's face —something Steve had left the round-up for, something he had to tell Laramie or die trying.

Laramie pulled to a stop to wait for Steve at the top of the hill. The news would tell him which way he needed to ride— Centennial Ridge, which was the closest town to the 50,000 acre McKinnon Ranch, or for the round up camp, or for the main house where Doctor Robert T. McKinnon lived.

Steve's horse puffed as he topped the hill and halted in front of Laramie. Steve took a deep breath and let it out, but no words came. Laramie tried not to think of who got hurt or even killed.

For all the rush, the words now seemed stuck in Steve's throat. He kept staring Laramie straight in the eyes, wordless.

This news was going to put to shame losing that fool steer in the brush.

Laramie spoke, his voice low and calm like always when one of his men had that panicky look in their eyes.

"What happened?" Laramie shifted in the saddle to better face Steve. "Something wrong with Doctor McKinnon?"

Steve settled himself then, gripping the reins with both

leather gloved hands. He slowly shook his head and swallowed. "No, but it's bad, Boss. It's Miss Rebekah."

Steve's tongue got stuck again, and it was just as well. Laramie felt all his senses leaving him.

Steve took a steadying breath. "Doctor McKinnon got word that something happened to her. He sent for you to get to the house right away."

Laramie didn't wait for his senses to come back. He turned the big gray horse and charged down the hill, Steve chasing after him.

Nothing could stop Laramie in this mission.

❦

WHEN LARAMIE CAME over the rise above the ranch house, he slowed Slate enough to begin cooling the big gray off. Dried lather from the hard ride flaked off Slate's dappled neck in the cool spring evening.

It was dark now, but a light shined from the open front door of the main house. The two-story mansion sat on the hill opposite of Laramie, and the light cast the outline of a stout, round figure standing on the porch.

It was too far away to make out anything other than the black silhouette, but Laramie knew it was Doctor Robert T. McKinnon. The ranch owner was waiting for him, hands sunk deep in his trouser pockets.

In the valley between Laramie and the house lay the barn, corrals, and the bunkhouse where the McKinnon ranch hands lived. Laramie Jones had been foreman of the ranch the past two years. It was only a short time before that when he'd gone to work at the ranch—on Doctor Rebekah LaRoche's recommendation.

Laramie loped down to the road that ran between the bunkhouse and barn, then up the section of road that led in front of the house. The nearby windmill that pumped water for the tank close to the house creaked in a slow turn.

It was the only sound Laramie heard as he came out of the saddle before the gray stopped. Laramie tossed the reins at Steve who caught them and kept the horses moving to cool them down.

Laramie's boots crunched on the gravel pathway that led to the house. He'd been right. Doctor McKinnon stood on the porch, watching for him, face drawn in a solemn frown.

The retired doctor was a portly, distinguished man with fine silver hair and a face chiseled from a lifetime of adventures—some good, some tragic. His skin was permanently tanned from years of hard work in the sun.

This evening, Doctor McKinnon was dressed in his usual white shirt, black string tie, and brown leather vest. But Laramie had never seen that kind of look in his eyes. One of fear and grief.

Now in the doctor's calm presence, Laramie felt himself coming undone. A fear he'd not known in years clawed at his insides.

"What happened, Doc?" Laramie swept off his hat and gripped it. "Is she dead?"

The doctor shook his head and turned to enter the house. Laramie was right behind him, closing the door. The fire in the parlor to the left of the foyer had died down, leaving the house with a chill. Laramie felt the cold in his bones like it was dead winter.

The doctor picked up a telegram from the entry table. Without a word, Doctor McKinnon offered it to Laramie, who took it and read the halting message aloud, "To Doctor Robert McKinnon, Centennial Ridge, Wyoming. Doc Beck kidnapped. Suspect Sancho Guerra. Will pursue. Cannot cross Mexican border. Thad Biggins, sheriff of Hagan."

Laramie read the telegram again, sure his eyes were playing a trick on him. "Kidnapped by Sancho Guerra?" He looked up to meet Doctor McKinnon's eyes. "I thought that bandit took off for Mexico after his gang was wiped out? And what was Miss Rebekah doing still in Hagan? I thought she was on her way home."

"So did I." Doctor McKinnon spoke for the first time, his normally deep voice cracked with the strain of speaking. He reached for the telegram and Laramie realized it was shaking in his own hands. Laramie hadn't shaken like that in years.

He let Doctor McKinnon have the telegram, then dropped his hand to rest on his holstered six-gun anchored on his right side.

Laramie let his thoughts come out as words. "That Sheriff Biggins mentioned he couldn't follow the bandit over the border. Sounds like that's where he thinks Guerra is headed with Becka."

Doctor McKinnon said nothing, and that said it all.

Laramie settled his hat down on his head, pulling it down tight in the front.

"I'll ride for her, Doc," Laramie said. "We'll get her back safe and sound, Lord willing."

He was sure the doctor's eyes watered but his voice, deep as Jacob's well, was steady. "It's dangerous, Laramie. I talked to Marshall Thorp when he brought the telegram out from Centennial Ridge. He told me Sancho Guerra's hideout in Mexico is a fortified valley that's been a hell-hole of bandits for decades. The Rurales have never been able to penetrate it, though they've tried for years. Once Rebekah is in there…"

Doctor McKinnon held Laramie's gaze, offering him a warning of what lay ahead. "We have to hope and pray that Sheriff Biggins and his posse are able to catch up with them before they cross the border."

Laramie licked his dry lips. "If not, you'll have to get a new foreman. I'm not coming back without her."

Doctor McKinnon was still for several seconds, then held out his hand to Laramie.

Laramie shook it firmly, turned, and left. He'd take his big gray horse on the first train south.

This might be the last mission he and Slate went on. But they couldn't fail like they did with the steer. Not this time.

CHAPTER 1

Traces of dawn speckled the vast Chihuahuan Desert with light, but did nothing to warm the air. Rebekah's teeth chattered as she kept her knees clamped against the horse's side to keep from falling off again.

She'd ridden with no hands when she was younger, but in her navy skirt and hands tied behind her back, it was almost impossible to stay upright in the saddle. Especially on the roadless desert terrain.

Her hair had come apart in the night, and hung stringy around her shoulders. It was so filled with dust and cockleburs, she wondered if it would have to be cut off.

Of course, that was the least of Rebekah's concerns. But it was better than dwelling on thoughts of whatever lay ahead.

Her horse, a stunning sorrel, was being led by Edgardo Guerra. This young man who defended her at the mission was the one who tossed her unwillingly into the saddle like a sack of grain.

They picked up a trot now and Rebekah stifled a gasp when she felt herself tilting. She pressed down hard in the stirrup and righted herself, her strength nearly gone after riding all night.

Edgardo glanced back at her, frowning, then faced forward again. He kept their horses in a straight line behind his father as Sancho Guerra led the way through the Chihuahuan Desert.

They had galloped part of the night, but the fourth time unseated Rebekah. Now Sancho Guerra set a steady pattern. Walk awhile. Trot. Walk. Trot.

Trotting was the worst. Rebekah had trouble finding her rhythm as they moved over the desert floor. Her horse stumbled more than once, but her sore shoulder from the fall motivated her to stay alert and in the saddle the best she could.

How long would the ride last? What lay at the end? If Jimmy were there, he'd quip something about being so scared he couldn't spit. But he wasn't there, thankfully.

Rebekah recalled their playful dinnertime conversation—could it possibly have been only twelve hours ago?—when she asked him when his birthday was. To her surprise, he didn't know. She urged him to pick a date, and they would celebrate it as his birthday from then on.

He was excited about the idea and went into a plethora of milestone dates he could pick; everything from the signing of the Declaration of Independence or Texas' secession from Mexico, to the day he met Rebekah. On that, he didn't know if he could wait a whole year for his first birthday party.

His litany of possibilities was daunting, and Rebekah finally told him she was going to retire to read for the evening. Jimmy said Sheriff Thad Biggins asked him to help tear down the scaffolding from the gallows where Pinto Diaz was hanged that morning. The town needed to put that business to rest.

Pinto Diaz's trial for Deputy Wallace's murder had been swift but not rushed. Rebekah pronounced Pinto Diaz's neck broken before treating two town patients that day. The dinner with Jimmy was a time to unwind and begin preparing herself mentally to return to Wyoming.

She should have left long before.

Instead, Rebekah found herself alone in her quarters when footsteps alerted her moments before the forced entry Sancho and Edgardo Guerra made into her quarters.

It would've been at least two hours before anyone knew she was missing, even if Jimmy stopped by her quarters that evening to bid her good night after tearing down the gallows.

Rebekah made sure there was evidence that it was Sancho Guerra who abducted her. In the struggle, she managed to break off a silver medallion from his vest and dropped it to the floor. Jimmy was observant. He would find it and know, then immediately alert Sheriff Biggins.

But Sancho Guerra knew this desert well and double-backed often. He had escaped across the border more than once in his notorious career.

Rebekah was shocked he had risked capture just to exact revenge on her. But there he was, doing just that.

The sun now began its ascent into the sky, turning the New Mexican sky blue and the earth around her red. Rebekah knew they were moving south through the Chihuahuan Desert, toward the Mexican border. Once they crossed it, there was no hope.

The walk/trot pattern continued through the morning as the sun not only warmed the desert but turned it hot. Rebekah swallowed, her mouth dry from breathing heavy and the heat. Neither Sancho nor Edgardo had taken a drink that she'd seen. They were born of the desert.

Around noon, Sancho held up one hand, halting his little caravan. When the movement beneath her stopped, Rebekah could feel every tremble and pain in her body.

But it was a relief to not be moving. She wasn't sure if she could hold on when they resumed.

Sancho swung his bay horse around and spoke quietly to his son. Edgardo nodded. Rebekah sensed there had been a shift in their relationship far from what she witnessed in the mission. Edgardo appeared fully dedicated to his father.

Edgardo handed his father the reins to Rebekah's horse and rolled his own horse back, spurring him into an instant gallop. He shot past Rebekah without a look.

Sancho tugged on her horse's reins to move the sorrel toward him. He looped her reins around the horn of his saddle and unhooked his canteen, looking at Rebekah with a hint of a smile.

Rebekah had never imagined what the anticipation of cool water could be. But she kept her face masked, determined not to show her fear and need.

Sancho Guerra took his time uncorking the canteen. He kept his eyes on her as he put the rim to his mouth, tilting it upward. He took a long, slow drink. Rebekah didn't want to watch the thin stream of precious water drip from the corner of his lips, but she couldn't break her gaze away from it.

Sancho slowly lowered the canteen and smiled. He spoke in English, his voice smooth with hardly a trace of malice. "Sister Rebekah, you are thirsty, no?"

Rebekah tried to swallow, but her throat was dried out. She didn't move, didn't acknowledge his taunting question. She was too dried out and scared to even spit.

His lips turned down into a mocking frown. "Oh, I forget! You do not speak English, do you, Sister Rebekah? Nor Spanish? I will teach you the words to say when you would like something to drink. They are, 'Please, Senior Guerra, I beg you to give me a drink of water.' Now, can you say those words, Sister Rebekah?"

Rebekah pressed her lips tight. Sancho would not give her a drink even if she begged.

Sancho cocked his head as though confused at her silence, then he smiled and re-corked the canteen. "Maybe later, yes?"

Hoofbeats sounded behind her, and within moments, Edgardo trotted up beside them. He spoke to his father rapidly in Spanish, telling him there was no sign of a posse.

Sancho Guerra directed them to the shade of a butte. Being shielded from the sun on her bare head was a tremendous relief. Sancho and Edgardo wore sombreros, but even Rebekah's darker skin wouldn't keep her from suffering the effects of direct sun for so many hours.

Once in the shade, Edgardo dismounted. He came to her horse's side and took hold of her waist, pulling her from the saddle. She slipped off faster than either expected and Rebekah hit the ground backwards with a cry.

She moaned as she tried to push herself to a sitting position, hand still tied behind her back. Sancho *tsked* at his son and spoke in English. "You must take more care with a señorita, my son."

Sancho lifted Rebekah by her shoulders. She held in tears at the pain in her shoulder, and in her inability to stand on her own. Sancho kept a grip on her and she raised her face to look up. He was smiling, very calm, but she knew he was a rattler poised to strike. The next time he struck at her, it would be for the kill.

Sancho pulled her through creosote bushes, their yellow blooms adding a delicate touch of beauty to the area, and lowered her to where she could rest against the red rock wall.

Edgardo began unsaddling the horses. He took great care in watering, putting their feed sacks on, and thoroughly rubbing them down. He had a natural way with horses that Rebekah wished translated to people. He would have bright potential if not for his father.

Sancho set about preparing a meal of hard tack and beans. Rebekah noticed he was putting together only two servings.

When Edgardo finished with the horses, the two bandits sat twenty feet away and began eating. Edgardo glanced at her, and she was almost certain there was a flash of remorse in his eyes. But he blinked and it was gone.

Rebekah closed her eyes and leaned her head against the coolness of the shaded rock. She turned to press her forehead against it, trying to bring her body temperature down. Though the bandits had brought her medical bag along, there was little in there that would help her. Except her pepperbox pistol.

What she must have was food and water, and it seemed these two had no intention of giving that to her.

Rebekah didn't recall falling asleep, but the next thing she knew, someone nudged her booted foot and she jerked awake. All her body ached, and her neck was so stiff she could hardly turn her head to look up at Edgardo towering over her. He had a disgusted look on his face, dampening the hope Rebekah had of mercy from him as she had received at the mission.

Of course then, she'd worn a nun's habit from a religion he greatly respected.

Edgardo got her to her feet. She stumbled forward, trying to get her legs to work. He guided her to the horses, which were saddled and ready to go.

It couldn't have been more than two hours since they stopped. Had the posse gotten any closer? They would have to rest as well, and waste time back tracking, whereas Sancho knew exactly where he was going.

They set out again, Rebekah struggling to stay in the saddle. They went on at the walk/ trot pace throughout the day, tramping around mesquite and yucca.

Rebekah's head got lighter with each hour. She could hardly keep her eyes open against the sun and the grit and the pain and the thirst and the hunger.

The desert swirled around, and then stopped when Rebekah hit the cracked earth. She let her eyes sink closed. As a medical physician, she knew death wasn't far away.

But someone scooped her up and put her back in the saddle. A rope went around her waist and bent her forward, the horn of the saddle stabbing her in the stomach. The rope tightened and moments later, they were moving again.

Rebekah tried to pull herself upright, but the rope held fast.

She struggled to breathe as her face pressed against the sorrel's hot neck. The scent of horse hair, sweat, and dust filled her nostrils.

If she didn't survive this, who would give Jimmy his first birthday party, or teach him how to read?

They rode late into the night, the pitch black darkness engulfing the Chihuahuan Desert and turning it cold once again. Rebekah shivered, trying to keep her body warm and remain awake. She wasn't sure if she was entirely successful, but her senses were aware when they finally halted around midnight.

The rope around her body loosened and she took one normal breath before she was pulled off to collapse on the ground. Edgardo half-carried her a short distance in the darkness, then lowered her to a rocky floor. She cracked open her eyes to see Sancho starting a fire not far away.

The thought of a warm blaze touching her cold body was inviting, but it also struck fear in her heart. If the pair was comfortable lighting a fire, it meant they no longer worried about the posse catching them.

Rebekah's tongue was swollen from the cold and lack of water, making her mouth feel stuffed full of cotton. She raised her head to get her bearings, but all she could see was a rock wall behind Sancho and above them. A cave?

Edgardo reappeared, squatting next to the fire as it blazed to life. He removed his gloves and spread his hands to enjoy the warmth.

It wasn't long before that warmth thawed Rebekah's lips enough for her to whisper, "Water...please."

Both Guerras looked over at her, and Sancho answered with his calm smile, "It seems our Doctor Rebekah speaks a little bit of English. She is working on saying the words I taught her. Remember them, Doctor Rebekah? 'Please give me water, I am begging you, Señor Guerra.'"

Rebekah laid her head on the solid rock ground and closed her eyes, trying to think of what she should do, what she could do. Nothing came to her thirsty mind.

Liquid splattered by her face and she felt moisture running over her cheek. Her mouth instinctively opened, tongue feeling for the precious liquid.

More dribbled. She opened her eyes to see Sancho standing over her, canteen tipped above her head. He let water run out and onto the ground by her face.

Rebekah tried to catch some of the falling water with her tongue, barely succeeding before he stopped.

"Tell us, *Doctor* Rebekah," he said, squatting beside her, "how long could a person live in a desert with no water?"

Edgardo appeared at his father's side, looking down at her, his eyes dark with an anger that made him unrecognizable to Rebekah.

He spoke, his voice deep with a coldness beyond the desert night. "You are not a doctor. You are a dog. You violated the holy cloth and the symbols I was taught to respect by my mother. It was the only thing I had left of her and you destroyed it with your lies and deception."

Rebekah turned her head, trying to look at him better, trying to comprehend his words. Up to this point, she thought it was Sancho who orchestrated her kidnapping and punishment for his gang being destroyed by the Mexican army. Now she realized it wasn't that at all. This was Edgardo's idea, to exact revenge for her trampling his mother's memory.

The realization came slowly to Rebekah, but there was no need to rush. The last few days of her life would be long and hard and then they would be over.

She'd never been afraid of death even though she didn't know what was beyond it. She'd lost that fear when her life lost its meaning. There was little point in living without meaning.

That was why she traveled the country and went into any situation, no matter the danger, searching for that meaning. She never dreamed it would lead her to this place.

Edgardo glanced at his father and spoke in Spanish. "My regret is that I could not make a plan to save Pinto, too."

Sancho swiped the droplets from the rim of the canteen and flicked them in Rebekah's face. He answered in English, "This was more important, my son."

⁂

REBEKAH FELT a blessed coolness over her eyes, bringing her back to consciousness. Someone was wiping a bandana over her face—gentle, caring. How was that possible? Thoughts started firing through her mind.

The Chihuahuan Desert. Sancho and Edgardo Guerra. Trotting horses.

Pain.

Had the posse found her? Jimmy?

Rebekah cracked open her crusty eyes to see a row of silver medallions stitched to a vest, illuminated by the dawn. One of the medallions was missing.

Her despair returned.

Sancho Guerra was on one knee beside her as he tipped his canteen over his bandana to allow more water to soak it. He wiped Rebekah's face again and she managed to suck one corner of the cloth into her mouth.

He chuckled. "See, Edgardo? The art of torture can take many forms."

Rebekah kept sucking on the bandana, drawing in as much moisture as she could. If only her physical body wasn't so overpowering in its demand to keep her alive, she would have refused it and died.

Whosoever drinketh of this water shall thirst again…

The scripture verse from the Gospel of John that she learned in childhood felt taunting in this thirsty land.

But she did want to live. She didn't know if that was possible, but she made up her mind then that she would do everything in her power to not die.

CHAPTER 3

The scene of the Mexican village before Rebekah might have been one of tranquility, if she could fully open her swollen eyes to see. After four days of hard riding, the trio had halted at the head of a road leading deep into a valley that sheltered a small village.

The day before, Rebekah sensed the moment they crossed the Mexican border, leaving behind any hope of rescue. If she wanted to survive this ordeal, she had to find a way on her own.

But she'd never doubted her abilities as much as she did while gazing at the valley before her, a natural rock fortress.

Three sheer walls of red granite surrounded the valley. The fourth wall, where they sat horseback, was unmanageable except for the road that came up it at an angle. There were guards standing atop rock formations on either side of the road, allowing them full view of anyone approaching from inside or out of the valley. This was the third set of guards Rebekah had seen.

When they had passed the first set of guards, Sancho told her there was only one way in and one way out of this place, called *Los Abrigos*, the shelter. No one entered or left without the valleys' permission.

The trio had it. The guards had already let loose shouts and were waving their hats to welcome Sancho and Edgardo Guerra back to Los Abrigos.

One of the guards jumped down from the rock and onto a horse, bareback. He galloped down the road into the valley, swinging his sombrero in a circle and whooping.

The illusion of a tranquil scene melted before Rebekah as figures in the valley ran out of buildings spread throughout the village.

She didn't have a chance to see anymore before Sancho trailed after the galloping man at a trot while Edgardo followed, pulling Rebekah's horse along. The horses were spent, but they had made it and miraculously, she had too.

Her hands were tied behind her back, though the bandits had untied her throughout the journey, and given her just enough food and water to keep her alive. The rope snagged on the raw flesh on her wrists, and she had blisters from clothing rubbing her skin and the saddle.

Rebekah had questioned her commitment to stay alive more than once. But she was alive and she would find a way to escape.

As celebratory gunfire sounded, Sancho looked back at his son with a wide grin. Edgardo returned it and they kicked their horses up into a wild gallop down the steep road.

Rebekah gasped, clenching with her legs, even though it was the rope wrapped around her that held her in the saddle. Still, she felt as if she would fly off and meet her death beneath trampling hooves.

Shouts of celebration joined the gunshots as Sancho and Edgardo Guerra reached the bottom in a cloud of dust and barreled through the village. It was a wild parade as the village people waved and blew kisses, or scrambled out of the way.

Sancho didn't slow the mad pace as he maneuvered across the valley floor, dodging farm implements, corrals, and worn adobe buildings. They started up another incline. Rebekah hadn't seen this rise in the valley, the hill they were now climbing and the mansion at the top.

It was like a medieval castle sitting on the highest point, over-looking the kingdom. A white terrace ran the length of the front, a short marble wall fencing it in. A variety of yucca scrubs trimmed it neatly in rosettes of evergreen, sword-shaped leaves and large white flowers.

Sancho and Edgardo brought the horses to a stop, facing the terrace. The dust settled and Rebekah blinked to clear her vision from her watering eyes. The air around her grew very still, and she realized the people, who had followed them up the road, were making a semi-circle behind them.

But they were silent now. Rebekah glanced back to see the joy on their faces were momentary. Now they looked exhausted, hungry. Fearful. They were all staring at the terrace.

Rebekah faced forward again to see an ancient woman coming across the terrace with natural grace as if she descended from centuries of royal breeding. She wore her silver hair in a tight bun held in place by a black shell comb inlaid with turquoise, and a gold tapestry dressing gown that revealed little of her skin. The skin that was exposed on her face and hands was soft; wrinkles revealed her age but in a dignified way. Her face looked timeless, as though she had always been. Perhaps that was why she didn't appear to move her feet as she glided across the terrace.

For the moment, the woman didn't even look at Sancho or Edgardo. Her eyes bore into Rebekah.

In that instant, Rebekah felt her destiny was tied to this woman, as though she had the power to give life as a mother would for her young. But there was nothing motherly in the woman's gaze, only the power. To give life or take it.

Sancho swung down from his horse, his back ramrod straight as always and his black charro suit looking in good condition despite the long journey. He strode up the center steps of the terrace and through an opening in the low marble wall. The ancient woman finally turned to him. He took her hand and bowed to kiss it.

Sancho straightened and she observed every inch of his face. When she nodded, he leaned forward and she offered her cheek for him to kiss.

They were close enough for Rebekah to hear him say, "I am home, *Abuelita*."

Rebekah felt a shock. This was Sancho Guerra's grandmother.

The woman observed Edgardo and then Rebekah. The first words she said to her grandson Sancho were, "Who is this woman?"

Sancho glanced back and for the first time since Rebekah met him, she saw he was under someone else's authority.

His smile was the same but tighter as he answered, "It is a long story, Abuelita. May I tell you at dinner?"

His grandmother moved nothing but her eyes, observing every part of Rebekah. Finally, the woman said to Sancho, "You will have her cleaned up. I do not wish dirt inside the *Grande Colina hacienda*."

While Rebekah contemplated the ridiculousness of the statement, surrounded by nothing but desert dust, Edgardo swung down from his horse. He untied the rope from around her and pulled her from the horse. He knew to hold onto her but she still collapsed to her knees.

The grandmother rattled something off to someone in the crowd and in a few moments, Rebekah was being lifted on either side by soft hands. Two older girls, one on either side of her, were supporting her as they maneuvered away from the horses.

Rebekah didn't know where they were taking her or what would happen next. She only knew anyplace was better than under Abuelita Guerra's stare.

CHAPTER 4

The next few hours were hazy. Rebekah was aware of being in a small adobe dwelling and stripped of her clothing to settle in a tub of cool water. As far as she knew, the dwelling was private with only the two girls. They set to work at scrubbing Rebekah down, but too harshly for her chafed skin. Rebekah let out a cry that let them know, and they eased up.

The girls didn't speak as they washed her hair and cleaned her wounds. She wanted to ask them to fetch her medical bag from Edgardo Guerra so she could treat her cuts, blisters, and raw wrists, but Rebekah couldn't get her lips to form words. They did give her sips of fresh water, which she was careful not to become greedy in.

After four days in the desert, she felt guilty about the water they used to bathe her. But at the same time, she recalled seeing more than one water well in the wild ride through the village. This was a desert oasis and through the bath and care of the two girls, Rebekah felt like it was paradise.

When she was bathed and in a robe, the girls tried to seat Rebekah at a table on a wood bench. She couldn't stay upright.

They moved her back to the bedroom where the tub of water was and settled her on a cot, propped up with a pillow.

They massaged red-orange sap over her wounds. The sap came from the branches of mesquite trees. Rebekah had used the remedy on patients before, but now she was the patient and content to let them treat her however they could.

One of the girls began emptying the tub while the other went to an adobe oven in the other room. She put a pot on the ledge and pulled tortillas from a basket.

Neither girl smiled. Their faces held the same expression Rebekah had seen of the other villagers, though tinted with innocence.

Rebekah sipped from the clay cup of water they left by her bed, savoring the clean coolness of it.

But whosoever drinketh of the water that I shall give him shall never thirst; but the water that I shall give him shall be in him a well of water springing up into everlasting life.

The scripture verses from her childhood wouldn't leave Rebekah's mind. She never, ever wanted to thirst again. What would it be like to have a well of water springing up in this place? Inside her?

By the time Rebekah finished the water, the other girl returned with beans wrapped in a tortilla. Rebekah would have preferred a bowl of chicken noodle soup back on the McKinnon Ranch and spring green grass as her view out her bedroom window. But this was a feast for now.

Rebekah forced herself to take a bite, chew, swallow, and take another bite. The other girl refilled her cup, and Rebekah washed down the last bite of her meal. Through the slits of her swollen eyes, she saw both girls sitting on the floor by the low cot, staring at her.

Rebekah tried to smile in appreciation but her swollen lips wouldn't form the bend. She managed a simple, *"Gracias."*

Both girls' eyes widened and they looked at one another, and back at her.

"You speak Spanish?" The older one of the two said. "We thought you were a foreign woman from an exotic place."

Rebekah tightened her lips, attempting to smile again. If only they knew how foreign she had felt most of her life.

"What are your names?" Rebekah asked in Spanish.

Even the few words exhausted her, but they were sufficient. The girls came alive.

The younger said, "I am Antonia Fuentes and this is my sister, Carmelita. We are servants for Señora Guerra. She is very, very surprised to see you, and to see her grandsons, Señor Sancho and Edgardo. Everyone thought they were dead. We heard they were overtaken and brutally slaughtered by the Mexican army. Señora Guerra has been preparing to avenge them."

It was a lot of Spanish words, but Rebekah's grasp of the language had improved the past few weeks, plus Antonia spoke slowly. She was so innocent to be in this place. Her brown eyes were soft and round, her long black braid pulled forward over her shoulder.

The older sister, Carmelita, was a few years older. She wore the under layer of her black hair down with the top layer braided into a crown on her head. Not quite a young girl, not quite a young lady yet. Such a vulnerable age.

Carmelita took Rebekah's plate and held it in her own lap. Rebekah realized she'd been about to drop it.

"What is your name, señorita?" Carmelita asked.

Rebekah thought of the various names she was called over the years—Becka, Miss Rebekah, Doc Beck. Recently, Sister Rebekah.

Mostly though, she introduced herself as Doctor Rebekah LaRoche. But that sounded ridiculous here.

She settled on, "My name is Rebekah."

The girls accepted this with a simultaneous nod. "Señorita Rebekah, you should sleep," Antonia said. "We will put cool cloths on your eyes. But you should sleep. Señora Guerra will send for you soon."

CHAPTER 5

Before Carmelita woke her, Rebekah's dream was of an explosion of wildflowers covering the hillside of the Omaha Reservation. Or maybe it was the McKinnon Ranch. One thing for certain was the man in a U.S. Cavalry uniform who rode to her rescue.

Rebekah struggled awake as Carmelita explained that the sisters needed to prepare her for dinner at the Grande Colina Hacienda—the great hill home.

Though Rebekah didn't imagine being able to hold herself upright more than five minutes on her own, she didn't have a choice if she wanted to stay alive in the valley of Los Abrigos.

The Fuentes sisters helped her dress in a soft yellow gown with cream lace trimmed in Spanish style. From the musty smell, Rebekah guessed the dress had been stored away for some time.

The sisters fussed over her, doing her hair in a soft twist at the back of her head and finishing it with a large Mother of Pearl shell comb. Rebekah had never been decked out in the wealth of bandits before.

The sisters helped her to her feet, the only part of her body that didn't feel chafed and sore. The tight corset the sisters inflicted on her held her back straight. She needed all the help she could get this evening.

The girls weren't doctors, but they had set Rebekah on the path to healing. She was far from being capable of escaping, but with the cold compresses and natural remedies the girls used, she could get through the next hour without collapsing.

Carmelita supported Rebekah as they made their way up to the hacienda from the adobe casita. There was a path that led to the open back door of the grand home which Rebekah could discern was the kitchen by the luscious smells.

Carmelita steered Rebekah to the left, around the house and to the side steps of the terrace. They mounted the steps and headed for the double front doors. Closer to them and her eyes fully open, Rebekah noted the carvings of ships and oceans on the ten foot doors.

Antonia went to the entrance and glanced back at Rebekah, her soft brown eyes looking like a doe knowing a hunter was about to take her life.

"Are you ready, Señorita Rebekah?" she asked softly.

Rebekah nodded, the tight skin of her neck adding to the pain in her body.

The wood doors swung open and Rebekah stepped across the threshold. She drew a quick breath of surprise. She was entering another world. Another century.

A history book. A fable.

Torches lit the twenty-foot-high walls holding up the long corridor. The torches were placed between Spanish conquistador-style armor guarding a palace fit for the king of Spain's home. At least in the 1500s.

Rebekah's mind started coming alive with questions of what this place was, how long it had been there, and how it survived for so long. One thing she didn't wonder about was how it was funded.

Antonia closed the door and tucked herself close to Rebekah's other side. She felt like a mother hen wanting to spread her wings and cover these girls.

What kind of life had they had? How long had they been stuck in this bizarre world?

The sumptuous aromas coming down the hall made Rebekah heady. Food far too rich for her sensitive stomach assaulted her nostrils.

When they reach the end of the corridor, the wall to her right ended, opening up to a dining hall. A heavy oak table, fifteen feet long, was spread with an inordinate amount of food. At the center of the lavish affair was a roasted pig, an apple clenched in his teeth as he glared at Rebekah.

She had a vision of Abuelita Guerra being in that pig skin, all pompous and bloated while not realizing what she truly was. Speaking of whom...

Abuelita Guerra was seated at the head of the table, Sancho on her right. They were the only two at the feast table set for three.

Rebekah wanted to laugh at the ridiculous amount of food for only a few people.

Sancho, dressed in a white charro suit with embroidered swirls in red, stood at her entrance. He bowed at the waist as he said across the room, "Welcome to the Grande Colina hacienda, Señorita LaRoche."

Abuelita Guerra never took her eyes off Rebekah. So, this was who Sancho Guerra inherited his unnerving stares from.

Rebekah took a steady breath. How she wanted to pray! Where was a fortifying scripture from her childhood now?

The Fuentes sisters, still flanking Rebekah, shrank behind her even as they helped her move down the long table.

Sancho came around his grandmother to pull out the chair on Abuelita Guerra's left. With the sisters' help, Rebekah seated herself gracefully. The girls skittered back to stand against the wall.

Sancho pushed Rebekah's chair forward then stepped away, his hand brushing her shoulder. Intentionally.

Abuelita Guerra's eyes shot to him then back to spear Rebecca. She had seen it as Rebekah felt it.

Sancho reseated himself and started to reach for the salad dish that was nearest him. Abuelita Guerra cleared her throat loudly and he halted with a demure smile. He spoke to Rebekah.

"I have been away from my grandmother's fine teachings too long," Sancho said in English. "When you are the leader of a group of men who do not know one end of a fork from another, you can be corrupted by them."

The word *corrupted* coming from Sancho Guerra was humorous, but Rebekah wouldn't laugh if she could. This was her inquisition, her moment of finding out whether she would live or die tonight.

Abuelita Guerra folded her hands in front of her on the table, and Sancho mimicked her, bowing his head. Abuelita Guerra swept her gaze from him to Rebekah, who folded her blistered hands, her bandage wrists hidden beneath the yellow silk sleeves of the gown, and closed her sore eyes.

As Rebekah listened to Abuelita Guerra recite a blessing over the food—it sounded as though she had spoken it the same way for decades—Rebekah wanted to add her own prayer. Instead, words spoken by Jesus came to mind.

And Jesus said unto them, I am the bread of life: he that cometh to me shall never hunger; and he that believeth on me shall never thirst.

The prayer wasn't lengthy and Rebekah joined in with a quiet *amen.*

Abuelita Guerra and Sancho crossed themselves then Sancho reached for the salad dish again. He offered it to his grandmother. Carmelita stepped forward and used two wooden paddles to scoop lettuce onto Abuelita Guerra's plate.

Carmelita's eyes darted as though counting the number of

leaves. She halted and Abuelita Guerra looked at her with cold eyes. Carmelita carefully removed a small purple leaf.

The grandmother picked up her fork and Carmelita stepped back. Rebekah held her frown. For this royal family to even have lettuce in a desert valley like this was a luxury.

Antonia began filling the gold goblets. Rebekah wondered if Spanish conquistadors had drunk from those goblets.

They began the meal in a silence that made Rebekah focus on one bite at a time. Carmelita had served her, and Rebekah was surprised at the wisdom she showed in the selections. She gave Rebekah gentle foods, rather than rich ones. She was a good nurse, something Rebekah very much needed.

After they finished the first course and the sisters began serving the second, Abuelita Guerra set her fork down and addressed Rebekah.

"My grandson told me how you deceived him and assisted in the killing and capture of my men," she said, the Spanish words sounding like death on her tongue.

Carmelita dipped a spoonful of beans onto Rebekah's plate, her hand trembling.

Abuelita Guerra continued. "He also told of how you are a woman doctor, yet you masqueraded as a holy sister. He wants his son, Edgardo, to have the privilege of executing you."

Carmelita dropped the bean bowl on the table. It didn't spill but did knock Rebekah's silver butter knife to the floor, drawing a sharp glance from Abuelita Guerra. Rebekah leaned forward to partially block the woman's view as Carmelita retrieved the knife.

Rebekah, mouth feeling as dry as when she was in the desert, didn't want to respond to the accusation or the threat. But she needed to draw attention from Carmelita.

"Señora Guerra, I did what I felt I must do," Rebekah said. "The life of a friend was threatened. Would you not have done the same in my place?"

Carmelita placed the knife back on the table and Abuelita Guerra's attention went back to Rebekah. Her eyes were afire.

"You will not dare presume what manner of woman I am, and what I would or would not do."

Abuelita Guerra leaned back as Carmelita added a chicken breast to her plate, but didn't shift her gaze away from Rebekah.

After several seconds of staring at one another, the silence in the room was crushing. Rebekah longed to find a place to rest, but she held herself in the chair as steadily as she could.

Finally, Abuelita Guerra spoke. "Upon examining your bag, I saw you have instruments and medicines that we did not yet possess. I am considering having your skills tested. There are those in Los Abrigos valley who will want you executed immediately. But one lesson they must learn is that time has no meaning in this place. It is something you will learn as well."

Abuelita Guerra nodded at Carmelita. "Remove the doctor to the guest quarters."

To Rebekah she said, "You are free to move about the valley. But you will not go up the road. I will send for you when I have made my decision."

Rebekah used her hands to push the chair back, though she was really pushing herself to her feet. Thankfully, Carmelita was immediately at her side and helping her get away from the table, away from Abuelita Guerra, away from Sancho, away from that ridiculous meal with its stuffed pigs.

CHAPTER 6

Jimmy had never been locked up in jail in his life. That was a source of pride for him, even at a young age, because plenty of boys his age knew the inside of a jail cell, and Jimmy could say he didn't.

But what was it the Word of God said about pride going before destruction?

Being locked up in a jail cell in Mexico wasn't complete destruction, but it felt like it to Jimmy when the guard clanged the cell door closed against Jimmy's continued protests.

"I'm telling you, I ain't going to do nothing against the law here! At least, not American law. If I've messed with one of yours, I'll make up for it, but you can't keep me here. I got to rescue a friend before it's too...late!"

Jimmy shouted the last word as the Mexican guard closed the door leading into the lawmen's office, blocking it from the sights and smells of the prisoners.

Jimmy didn't blame the guard for leaving so quick. Not only did the man likely not understand a word Jimmy said, the odor in the prisoner area was enough to drive anyone out.

Jimmy rattled the cell door in frustration. He'd barely crossed the Mexican border and made it through two villages, trying to find where Sancho Guerra's hideout might be, when he landed in a place called Golden and the local law snatched him up.

Hearty laughter sounded behind Jimmy and he jerked around to see a heavy-set man settled in the back corner, grinning at him with yellow teeth. What teeth the man had left, anyway.

It didn't look like he'd lost them in fights, though. More like too much whiskey drinking. Smelled like it, too.

The man laughed again and hollered something in Spanish at Jimmy. They were the only ones in the large communal cell, so there was hardly a reason to shout.

Jimmy frowned and shrugged. He didn't know what the man said. Didn't want to know. If he didn't get out of there soon, who was going to rescue Miss Rebekah? Was she even still alive?

"Yes, she is!" Jimmy hollered at the wall and banged his fist on the cell door behind him.

The man chuckled and stroked his mustache that drooped clear to his shoulders. He shouted something at Jimmy again and laughed.

Jimmy glanced around the cell for a way to escape. He'd heard cowboys brag about breaking buddies out of jail after a drinking binge, but Jimmy didn't have those kinds of friends. Especially not in Mexico. There was only one Friend he had who could help him and Miss Rebekah.

Jimmy ignored his cellmate, who kept talking to him in Spanish, and went to one of the cots furthest away. He knelt by it, clasped his hands together, rested his elbows on the dirty blanket, and closed his eyes. He didn't know whether to pray for Doc Beck or himself first to get out and rescue her. Looked like he'd have time for both.

He began praying while the man laughed harder behind him.

CHAPTER 7

Rebekah spent the next three days in a plush guest room in the hacienda wondering how often the suite was used. What sort of people were voluntary guests of the Guerras?

Carmelita brought meals to Rebekah and treated her wounds each day. Rebekah learned the girl had worked inside the house the past two years whereas Antonia only started a few months ago, and was still unnerved every time she stepped through the front doors.

Rebekah understood that feeling. There was a sense of evilness emanating from the walls, echoing loud whenever footsteps passed by her door. Each time, Rebekah wondered if Abuelita Guerra was sending for her to have her executed; or if she was ready to test Rebekah about becoming the village doctor.

After three days under Carmelita's treatment, Rebekah felt well enough to venture beyond those walls. While she didn't feel strong enough to attempt an escape, she could scope out the valley, and meet the inhabitants to see if she could find sympathy among them. A woman as harsh as Abuelita Guerra likely had close enemies.

Rebekah headed out of the room on the third morning and down the corridor where she found a side door to leave through.

The warmth of the morning told her she didn't want to be out past ten. She was quite done with suffering in the desert heat for now.

The road leading down from the hacienda at a slant tested Rebekah's sore muscles, but she made it to the bottom without stumbling. The layout wasn't so unlike Doctor McKinnon's home on the ranch in how it sat on a rise overlooking the barn and bunkhouse. But she never received hostile looks like she did there at Los Abrigos.

At a blacksmith anvil under a thatched awning, two men were making horseshoes. They halted and stared at her, eyes dark under long black bangs. Were they related to any of the bandits killed by the Mexican army with Rebekah's help?

Across and to the left from the men, a cluster of women were shucking corn. They knelt around a pile of dried corn cobs, rubbing cobs on flat, textured stones. The women stopped talking and watched Rebekah, their expressions showing their suspicion.

Perhaps venturing out of her room hadn't been a good idea.

Rebekah made it through that area and to a large corral where a herd of horses meandered. They spotted her and several came over to the fence, bobbing their heads over the top rail. Rebekah stepped close, inhaling their fresh scent.

A dappled gray dropped his head over the rail and nudged Rebekah's hand. A thrill of delight went through her and she rubbed the back of her hand against his warm nostrils, then stroked his dappled face.

Perhaps she'd found an ally. She leaned close and whispered, "You remind me of a friend's horse. Would you take me away from this place if I asked?"

The horse blew through his nostrils and pressed his head against her. Rebekah smiled and gave him another pat. She reluctantly moved away from the corral. She needed to keep looking for allies.

She circled a casita. To her amazement, the laughter of children met her ears. As she came around the corner, she found a backyard where a boy and girl played with a white puppy, taking turns chasing it and it chasing them. A woman sat on the back stoop, mending, while a man worked a round stone, sharpening a knife blade. Several knives lay on a table beside him, along with three hoes and a machete, as though it was his job to sharpen everything in the village.

The children halted and gaped at Rebekah. The woman looked up, along with the man. The family stared at her, silent.

Rebekah backed away. What sort of place was this that could hold her hostage while children played carefree?

She continued her slow trek through the village, imprinting the sporadic roadways and buildings in her mind. It didn't appear to have any sort of master design, just pieces added when they were needed for who knew how long.

Though Rebekah appeared to be wandering, she did have a final destination in mind. She was getting as close to freedom as she could.

She reached the bottom of the road that led out of the valley and stared up it.

The road appeared built by engineers who knew what they were doing. She guessed it was 300 yards, and there were no brush or boulders along the way to make a clandestine trip to the top. No shadows to hide in, nor a trench to crawl through. The right side of the road was sheer rock face while the left was a steep drop into the valley.

The dappled gray horse could gallop it in under a minute—which was ample time for someone with moderate shooting skills to get in several deadly shots at her.

"You must not think such thoughts, Señorita."

Rebekah swirled at the sound of a gravelly voice speaking the

Spanish words behind her. A whisper of an old man stood there, looking as though he had existed in that spot for ages, like a stone statue from another era.

He wore a wide sombrero and a faded wool poncho despite the warming morning. A wood cane in his hand looked like an extension of his body, a third limb that kept him upright. His face, the color of stained oak, appeared carved from the earth, reminding Rebekah of the Indian elders in her life. Her heart stung with a longing for home.

The old man gestured toward the road behind her. "You must not think such thoughts. Those who try to reach the top without leave always fail."

Rebekah felt her tense shoulders go slack, unable to hold back the feeling of defeat. Anyone who had seen her staring at the road knew what she was thinking, but it didn't matter. It was impossible to escape by simply riding up the road.

The old man held up a gnarled finger and crooked it at her. "Come, you should have a cool drink of water and a siesta. You are very, very tired."

This old man was very, very right. Despite days of rest, the hard ride through the Chihuahuan Desert and all she had endured in the weeks before were catching up to Rebekah. It started with the Baxter brothers holding her at their ranch near the Palo Duro Canyon and escaping from there with Jimmy.

But really, she could trace her fatigue to before that—working long hours at the hospital in Amarillo; before that, her work in Indian Territory; her mission before that; and before that, and before that.

When was the last time she truly rested? Even on her last visit to Doctor McKinnon's ranch, she hadn't relaxed in her spirit. Her soul was as restless as her body. It had been since she'd been driven off the Omaha Indian Reservation.

And now, there she was at Los Abrigos, the shelter for bandits, a place she certainly couldn't rest.

The old man began shuffle-walking back toward the village. Rebekah joined him, taking half steps to match his pace. She asked, "What is your name, Señor?"

"My name is Gabino Fuentes."

A jolt went through Rebekah and she glanced at him. He was slightly shorter than her when walking hunched over his cane.

"That is the same last name as the two sisters who work in the Grande Colina Hacienda," she said. "They have cared for me well."

The old man kept his steady pace. "I know this. Antonia has told me stories of who you are, though she knows very little. Antonia and Carmelita are my granddaughters. I am not glad for them to work at the hacienda. Only their father, Martín, is."

They reached his casita and the shade of its dirt porch, the overhang supported by rough-cut posts.

Gabino Fuentes pointed to two chairs situated outside the open front door. "I will bring water."

Rebekah took a seat in one of the chairs, aware that she was in full view of much of the village activities. People went about their business, though she noticed glances her way. What kind of power, if any, did this old man hold among these people? Was he as evil as the Guerras? It was possible, but Rebekah sensed a different spirit in him.

Gabino Fuentes returned with a wooden tray shaking in his hand. Rebekah quickly stood and took the tray, noting the two pottery glasses of water and the pitahayas—fist-sized flaming pink and green fruit harvested from cactus.

"Gracias," the old man said. Relieved of his burden, he shuffled a few more steps and sank into the other chair. Rebekah set the tray on a small table as she reseated herself. She handed him a water and took a long drink from hers.

She needed to find a canteen and keep it with her. In fact, she needed many supplies. If by some miracle she made it to the top of the road and past the three sets of guards, she would need supplies to see her to the border, or to the nearest town.

But what if the closest towns were under the Guerras' control? Rebekah's best chance was to head north for the border.

Rebekah settled in to the hard chair and remained quiet as she peeled a pitahaya, slowly revealing the white flesh inside.

She knew only a little of the Mexican culture, but if the elders were anything like those among her people, she was in for a long sit on the porch in silence.

She finished peeling the pitahaya and handed it to Señor Fuentes before taking up another one to peel.

Gabino Fuentes held his fruit in one arthritic-ridden hand and began speaking. "You are a wise and well brought up young woman. You must have the patience of Job to sit with a boring old man like me."

Rebekah let her gaze roam the village scene before her, people going about their slow business in this strange setting. "Have you been here all of your life, Señor Fuentes?"

He chuckled. "All of my life and then some, or so it feels. I have lived my life, watched my son Martín live his, and now my granddaughters. Antonia and Carmelita, they have never known the world beyond this one. If I had known that would be the future of the children from my body, I would have run away from this place; from my father and his friend, Señor Thomas Guerra."

Rebekah resisted the temptation to turn loose her bottled up questions at the speed of a Gatling gun. She took a bite of her peeled pitahaya. The strong flavor set her senses on edge. She felt old Gabino was watching her, but not like the Guerras did. It was as if he was forming his narrative based on who she was—the mark of a true storyteller.

"It was many, many years ago," Gabino Fuentes went on. "Señor Thomas and my father never intended it to become this bandit-hole. They were angry at the Mexican government and wanted separation from it—a shelter. He and my father worked together. They built this place. My father engineered that road you are contemplating dying on."

Rebekah closed her eyes briefly then reopened them, watching the village as Gabino Fuentes continued the story of Los Abrigos.

"They made this place impenetrable so that we could live in peace. Señor Thomas and my father, and ten other young families, threw in their lot with us. I was fifteen at the time. We were all very close, and trusted one another implicitly. But their mistake was in not placing checks and balances in the power structure. They thought the people here knew better than to corrupt this garden of Eden. But there is a serpent in every Eden, sí?

"When my father died in a riding accident—far too young for such a strong man—Señor Thomas Guerra was solely in charge. But he was so busy fortifying this place he did not realize what his young daughter was scheming."

Rebekah had some trouble following the long narrative in Spanish, but she was certain she understood this part. She swallowed. "That would be Sancho Guerra's grandmother?"

Gabino Fuentes drew in a deep breath, past the point of lung capacity it seemed to Rebekah. He finally let it out slowly, ending in a puff.

"Sí. Isabel Guerra was my age when we moved here, but quiet, and I paid her little mind. As the years went by and I struggled to make a life here, she was building allegiances among the families. It wasn't until our hunting party of young men returned with the Mexican army chasing them that we realized what she had done—sent them out to steal a shipment of gold from the government. We defended our young men, making us all wanted criminals. Señor Thomas tried to set the village back to rights, but he was ill and died within a few months. I was preoccupied with raising my own family and didn't realize how Isabel positioned herself as queen of the village. When she had one of our own people executed for dissidence, and the others allowed it, I realized how complete her control was. She even retained her father's name when she married. Ah. Her husband. He was a good man—while he lived." Señor Fuentes sighed. "My own health was failing and my son was starting his family. He wanted peace above all, and convinced me to turn a blind eye to Señora Guerra and her ways. But her ways must end."

Rebekah held her breath, trying not to show the hope those simple words gave her. During her time of recovery, she thought about how the blow of losing so many men at the mission in New Mexico must have hurt the valley. Were things starting to crack in the village? Was Abuelita Guerra losing control?

Señor Fuentes took a long sip from his water, his hand shaking from fatigue and the many years of his hard life.

Rebekah found herself looking him over with a practiced eye —no longer seeing him as the enemy nor a potential ally, but as an old man who had health conditions she might be able to help with.

She tapped his untouched pitahaya. "Please eat this, Señor. It will give your body a boost."

He rested the fruit on his leg with a chuckle. "I forget you are a doctor. But please, Señorita, do not waste your medical skills to keep me alive. I would most welcome death."

To stop her mind from running through the possible remedies she could treat him with, Rebekah let her eyes sweep across the village again.

The sound of clipped footsteps brought her attention to the left to see a tall man striding toward the porch. His right arm was in a sling, his hand bandaged. He had that frightened-angry look that she recognized, similar to many faces Rebekah saw in this place. His eyes went from her to the old man who frowned at the sudden approach.

The tall man spoke rapidly. "Papá, why are you speaking with this woman? She is condemned and will soon die."

Gabino Fuentes lifted his head higher to look up at his son who towered over him.

"Martín, if she is to die soon, I have had the honor of preparing her last meal."

Martín Fuentes glared at Rebekah. He waved his hand as if shoeing her away like a horse fly. "Leave. Leave! Leave my family, my daughters. If I hear you are filling Carmelita and Antonia's minds with nonsense of the outside world, I will kill you myself."

Rebekah set aside her cup of water and rose. She doubted this man possessed the spine to do her harm, but he was desperate—and desperate men were capable of most anything.

She looked down at Gabino Fuentes. "Thank you for the refreshments, and the story. There is very little in this village for a condemned woman to do."

Rebekah headed back toward the Grande Colina Hacienda on the hill, away and opposite of Gabino Fuentes' dwelling. Opposite in every way.

CHAPTER 8

Rebekah spent the next morning with the sisters and the cook in the Grande Colina Hacienda kitchen, preparing mountains of food. With dinner in Rebekah's room the evening before, Carmelita informed her that there would be a fiesta, a grand celebration for the safe return of Sancho and Edgardo Guerra.

Rebekah suspected the fiesta was meant to distract grieving families from the men who hadn't returned. Although, according to Carmelita, many of the bandits had been mercenaries who joined Sancho and weren't from the valley. But not all.

Carmelita grew quiet at this, and Rebekah wondered how many Carmelita valued were lost in the mission raid that Rebekah helped with. Did the Fuentes sisters hold ill-feelings toward her for it? They didn't seem to, but then, they were still fascinated by the foreign woman.

The fiesta was likely Abuelita Guerra's attempt to re-strengthen her power over the disgruntled people who had expected riches to return along with their army. According to Carmelita, the people in the valley worked hard to grow food, make clothing, and raise herds of sheep, cattle, and horses. The Guerra family's responsibility was to bring in supplies and money.

It seemed Sancho and Edgardo had returned penniless from the raid, which, although people celebrated their return at first, were questioning what the leadership would do to support them now.

Abuelita Guerra would probably make some sort of announcement while everyone's hearts were merry and gain their recommitment to loyalty and whatever her next scheme was.

Hopefully, whatever Abuelita Guerra had planned to cheer the people up wouldn't include Rebekah's execution.

Rebekah held out hope that the people would see her value as a medical doctor. If she could treat enough people in the village, from helping with childbirth to bandaging bullet wounds, she would gain friends there. It would be a long, slow process, but there was no help coming from the outside. Being the doctor of Los Abrigos would give Rebekah time to plan a real escape, one that didn't involve her getting killed.

Meanwhile, Rebekah decided to make herself useful with helping prepare the generous feast that Abuelita Guerra was going to bestow on her people.

The food, which the hacienda cook started the evening before, was ready by noon. Rebekah went with the Hacienda servants carrying it down to the center of the village where several tables were set up for the feast.

The celebration was getting underway within the horse corral. The horse herd had been removed and temporary chutes built inside, along with grandstands around it. They were having a rodeo.

As Rebekah approached the table with her large bowl of corn, one of the chutes opened and out busted Edgardo, riding a bronc as onlookers whistled. He rode the bucking horse around the corral once before rolling and landing on his feet in a billow of dust.

He removed his sombrero and swirled it in an elaborate bow, grinning as the audience cheered. Rebekah felt a pain in her heart. He looked like the happy young man he should be at his age.

Edgardo took another turn and Rebekah caught the kind smile he cast Carmelita's way. The girl was standing near the chutes, her blush showing despite her rebozo, a long shawl covering her head.

The moment came and went in Rebekah's heart when the crowd realized the food was there. She quickly took several steps back as the men converged on the tables.

There was no order to the meal. They grabbed tortillas and made burritos, eating chips and salsa as they moved from table to table, laughing.

It was a blend of people raised by bandits with a semblance of their dignity still intact.

Rebekah thought the fiesta would end before dark, but Abuelita Guerra apparently intended the celebration to go into evening. The woman spent the day seated on a red velvet chair atop a high platform, an awning shading her in the afternoon heat. Antonia stood on one side of the platform, looking frightened as she fanned the queen of the valley.

As darkness fell, children set off fireworks, shrieking and laughing. There was music, tambourines and guitars and shouts throughout the village.

The day before, four of the village men returned from a successful raid in a nearby town. They brought back a few dry good supplies, and two cases of whiskey. Torches lit up the valley as the people indulged in dance and song and drink.

Abuelita Guerra was sealing the cracks in her domain.

Rebekah kept herself away from the excitement as much as possible, opting to stay close to the food tables. It was disheartening to see Carmelita dancing with Edgardo. They looked as happy as young people should, but what kind of future could they have in Los Abrigos?

As the evening continued growing wilder, Rebekah returned to the hacienda with the cook for more food. Rebekah contemplated retiring to her room, knowing where the drinking would ultimately lead.

But the cook insisted she carry a pot of beans down to the tables. Rebekah would slip away after that.

Staying in the shadows of adobe dwellings, Rebekah settled a pot on the table farthest from the drinking.

"Doctor Rebekah."

She jerked back, looking up to see Sancho Guerra approaching her.

Their eyes met and she knew she wouldn't be able to avoid him. She reached for a tortilla as though to make herself something to eat.

Sancho pressed his fingertips against the back of her hand, forcing the tortilla back into its container.

"Will you permit me this dance?" he asked.

Rebekah felt like he was choking her again. She gasped for a breath while saying the first thing that came to mind.

"I do not wish to."

Wrong words. Sancho's face darkened to that tint he had moments before his hands had gone around her throat.

But now he smiled, amused.

"Doctor Rebekah, when your captor asks you to dance...you accept."

Sancho walked his fingers across her hand then wrap them around hers. He pulled her around the table that had separated them.

Rebekah shuffled her feet, hoping he would see how wooden they were and not want to embarrass himself with her as a dance partner. One thing she knew— Sancho was very aware that people watched him. He capitalized on every moment of it.

Rebekah got a glimpse of Abuelita Guerra watching from her platform situated near the dancing. The woman was frowning.

Sancho noticed Rebekah's gaze and glanced over at his grandmother. He tugged Rebekah into his arms and swung her into the dance.

She almost went down, but he steadied her as he leaned close and said above the sounds of guitar and singing, "My grandmother has forgotten what it is to be young and filled with passion."

Rebekah yanked her hand out of Sancho's and twisted away from his grip. She didn't look at him, not at Abuelita Guerra, not at the bandits around them wearing crossed ammunition belts at the celebration.

She strode away from the fiesta, aware of people who saw the incident. She had defied Sancho in front of his entire village. A bullet could strike her in the back any second.

When she made it to the kitchen door of the hacienda, Rebekah took a deep, shaky breath. Her punishment would come later.

Maybe days, maybe weeks, maybe months. Abuelita Guerra said time held no meaning in Los Abrigos.

CHAPTER 9

Jimmy's stomach growled like usual when the guard brought his meal one evening. He was frightfully hungry—as usual—but it was partly because of the awful food they served in that jail. He could hardly eat it each of the three days he'd been there, but he had to and fast, before his cellmate finished his own portion.

The guard slid two trays through the slot at the bottom of the bars. Jimmy grabbed his quick. He was never the smartest in a bunch, but he was a fast learner. He woofed down the plate of beans and tortilla before his cellmate started looking for it.

Then they did like usual. Sat on the cots on opposite sides of the cell and stared at each other.

From what Jimmy could make out, his laughing, long-term cellmate's name was Pedro, and was in jail for busting up the local cantina. Other men were in and out of the jail, but Jimmy guessed Pedro couldn't pay his fine and had to serve longer time.

Jimmy still didn't know why he'd been arrested himself, and there wasn't anyone who could talk English to explain it to him.

With nothing but time on his hands, Jimmy thought about how silly he was to get all excited about Doc Beck going to celebrate a birthday for him. He recalled something from the Bible that stuck with him, something a Preacher in it said about the day of a man's death meaning more than the day of his birth. If Jimmy died helping Miss Rebekah, that day would sure mean more than any birthday.

After staring blankly at Pedro for awhile, like they had every day for the past three days, Jimmy sighed and slid off the cot onto his sore knees. He'd experienced saddle soreness, foot soreness, and head soreness, but never knee soreness. Maybe he should make that a habit.

Jimmy bowed his head and closed his eyes. "Lord, I'm asking You again to get me out of here to save Miss Rebekah, or else, You save her. She's been awful good to me, Lord, and I haven't done nothing for her. She can take care of herself but I don't figure she'd mind if You helped a whole lot right now. I'm scared for her, Lord, scared what that Sancho fellow might do to her, even tonight. Lord, please, I'm begging You, look out for her, would You?"

Something brushed Jimmy's arm and he jerked back, opening his eyes. Pedro was lumbering beside him, swaying like he was going to fall on Jimmy.

Jimmy quickly put his hands on the man's backside and helped him lower himself to sit on the cool cell floor.

They sat cross legged staring at each other awhile. Then Pedro gestured, making a sign of folding his hands as he spoke. He looked at Jimmy, a deep question in his eyes.

Jimmy nodded. He didn't know how, but he understood. Pedro wanted Jimmy to pray for him.

Jimmy wasn't sure if it mattered that he prayed in a different language than the man spoke. He did want Pedro to know his next prayer was for him, so he tentatively put a hand on the man's shoulder. He'd been a little scared of the big man in the cell with him, remembering the giant Pinto Diaz slinging him around like a rag doll.

But Pedro was asking for prayer, so Jimmy closed his eyes again. "Lord, I can't understand this man, but You can. You know how he's hurting right now and what he needs. Most of all, I know he needs You. I'm asking You to send someone who can show him how to follow You."

Jimmy peeked up to see what Pedro was doing. The man bowed his head and began muttering in Spanish. Then he paused, took a deep breath, and began again. This time, Jimmy was sure he heard the man say the words, *Señorita Rebekah*.

Good. There were at least two praying for her now.

CHAPTER 10

A dog barked as Laramie Jones rode into the otherwise quiet Mexican village set in the Chihuahuan Desert.

By the pitch of its tone, the dog was a small one, its yapping high and nervous. Probably what Laramie's voice would sound like if he tried to speak.

He guided his big gray gelding at a slow walk up the only street of the village, his eyes darting back-and-forth between the adobe buildings. Only one person should know he was coming, but a lone man riding into a border town like this was risky.

Something Laramie had in his favor—he didn't look like a greenhorn. He wore two six-guns tied down and an ammunition belt across his chest. His face was unshaven for the past five days, and his hair was already overdue for a cut when he left the McKinnon Ranch in Wyoming. The edges had a curl now.

All in all, it wasn't a wonder he made it to the cantina without anyone challenging him.

Laramie swung down from the saddle and tied Slate to a hitching post. There were bandit-eyes watching him from the shadows, but as long as they didn't make any quick moves, he wouldn't either.

He crossed the dirt porch and went through the swinging doors of the cantina. The smoke-filled inside was as quiet as the rest of the village. Nothing happening but a game of poker in one corner, and another group of men eating a late dinner at a table close to the door. They were dusty and armed to the teeth.

Every head in the room raised a touch to observe Laramie, then the men returned to their game and meal. But he knew they wouldn't stop watching him, and he planned to do the same.

A polished bar ran alongside the right of the room. The middle-aged man who tended it was the one who watched Laramie the longest.

Laramie ran his hand along the smooth surface of the bar as he followed it down to the bartender. Midway down, Laramie was able to make out a slumped over figure at a table in the shadowy corner.

Laramie kept sliding his hand down the bar, past the tender. He let his hand drop off the end of the bar and ambled over to the table. Pulling out a chair to the man's left put them side-by-side to where Laramie could see the whole room like his friend could. He turned the chair backward and straddled it as he sat.

The barkeep came over and Laramie said, "Tequila."

Though he wasn't a drinking man, having something sitting in front of him could come in handy, especially if anyone approached and he needed to start a fight.

The man beside him had his hat low as he hunched over a mug, eyes down.

After the barkeep set Laramie's drink in front of him, the other man took a sip of his own and spoke English in a quiet voice. "The boy you wired about is being held in Golden, not many miles from here. The sheriff took him into custody before he got himself killed, wandering around Mexico looking for Sancho Guerra."

Laramie put one hand on his leg, partly turning to his old friend, Fernando Contrera.

"Good," Laramie said. "Best to leave him there. I'll pick him up on my way out."

Contrera half-smiled as he took another sip, saying into his mug, "Still the old capitán. Confident as ever when he's on a mission. No matter that not all of his missions have been successful."

Laramie knew Contrera didn't mean the comment to be offensive. He was just reminding Laramie what a dangerous situation they were in and to take heed.

But there was no other way. When Laramie reached the town of Hagan, he found Sheriff Thad Biggins and his posse returned from trying to catch Sancho Guerra before he reached the border with Doc Beck. He told Laramie how the boy, Jimmy, had kept going despite the warnings of the dangers across the border from bandit villages and hideouts, not to mention the deadly desert itself.

That was when Laramie wired his friend in the Rurales, Fernando Contrera, about the trouble and asked for the boy to be picked up. Contrera offered to join him on this mission that could get them killed.

It was a fool's errand and they both knew it, but that kind of knowledge never stopped them when they served together in the U.S. Cavalry. Their last fool's errand got them dishonorably discharged.

Laramie shook away the memory and said, "I'm not figuring on failing in this mission, my friend. That valley is holding an American woman, and I want her back."

Contrera pushed his sombrero up enough to scan the room. "There is a man from Guerra's valley, Los Abrigos, here now. Seated to the right of the card dealer at the poker table. He thinks I sell weapons to renegades, and is the only contact I have in the valley. After routing Sancho Guerra at the mission school, the Mexican army is most anxious to break into Los Abrigos at last. I do not believe I have sufficiently gained the man's trust, but now with your news, I see I can wait no longer to make my move into the valley."

Laramie tightened his grip on his leg. "I'm not asking you to risk your life."

The half-smile came to Contrera's face again. "It is no different than former times, yes?" He pulled his sombrero down close to his eyes again, still observing the room as he added solemnly, "We will get her out, my friend. I have a plan."

"I hope it's a good one."

The man sipped from his mug, foam sticking to the black whiskers of his mustache. "As do I."

He looked at Laramie from the corner of his eyes, the brim of his sombrero tipped down so that no one could tell which way he was looking. "I am anxious to meet this Doc Beck," Contrera said. "You must love her fiercely to risk all for her."

"I reckon it's natural to care for someone who saved your life —more than once."

Contrera nodded, and touched a short white scar on his jaw. "I know this feeling."

Neither of them needed to talk about the times Laramie saved Fernando Contrera's life. Just like Laramie didn't need to say anything else about Doctor Rebekah LaRoche, his oldest and truest friend.

CHAPTER 11

Because Carmelita and Antonia quartered in one of the casitas near the Grande Colina Hacienda but on the hill above the rest of the inhabitants of the village, it gave the Fuentes sisters the best of both in this eerie world. It also gave Rebekah a refuge like it had her first day in Los Abrigos.

Two weeks into her captivity, Rebekah found herself seated outside of the sisters' quarters with Carmelita and Antonia as they wove on a loom. Antonia was quite an artisan in making serapes and blankets. She helped Rebekah get started on a blanket that Rebekah hoped to not finish.

Since the fiesta last week, Rebekah did her best to stay clear of Sancho Guerra as she secretly gathered supplies for an escape. There was no indication that Abuelita Guerra was going to trust her as a doctor, and that didn't leave much else but death for Rebekah. Or worse.

Rebekah focused on the dyed red wool she wove through the loom. She had done similar work in her growing up years and found it peaceful for her mind.

While they worked, Antonia peppered Rebekah with questions about where she was from and what her life was like before coming to the village. When Rebekah told them she had traveled around the United States by train, Antonia froze with the ball of green yarn she was rolling.

She gaped at Rebekah. "Please, Señorita, tell us what a train is like."

Rebekah was surprised at the intensity of the question. She decided to answer with one she had. "Have you never traveled by train, Antonia?"

The sisters looked at each other and giggled. Carmelita shook her head.

"Señorita Rebekah, neither my sister nor I have ever left this valley. Our papá barely has. Though we have heard there is a large, large world out there with many, many people and civilizations and history, I do not know whether to believe it is true. But then, here you are. Perhaps we will believe you."

Rebekah stared at the sisters, trying to comprehend their isolated lives. They had never known anyone or anything beyond the walls of this valley. If only she could take them with her when she escaped—if she made it.

"Tell us more, Señorita," Antonia pleaded.

Rebecca cast about in her mind for stories to tell them. Of grand cathedrals in Europe? Washington DC, their neighbor's capital? Her own people, the Omahas?

But she felt drawn to share something that applied directly to their lives.

"In the United States of America, there are many laws," she began slowly. "There are men who arrest those accused of breaking the laws, and a judge and jury decides if they are innocent or guilty and how to punish them. It is an imperfect system but it is intended to keep people who live justly protected from those who do not."

Antonia stared at her, trying to understand the meaning of Rebekah's words. But Carmelita stiffened.

"It is most imperfect, Señorita," Carmelita said. "Those you speak of with the law are the ones we must protect ourselves from. They hate us because we are better than they."

Rebekah wanted to change the subject, but something prompted her to continue. "As I said, it isn't perfect. In Hagan, New Mexico, there was a trial for one of the men from Los Abrigos here. He was falsely accused of murdering a girl. Thanks to one law man's determination to see justice done, the real killer was caught and found guilty rather than Pinto Diaz."

Antonia dropped the ball of yarn. It hit the ground and rolled.

Rebekah scooped it up and looked at the girls who stared at her, mouths agape. Carmelita recovered first.

"Señorita, Pinto Diaz is our mother's brother. Our uncle. He... he always brought us gifts and extra food." Carmelita blinked, her eyes reddening with tears. "He survived the slaughter at the mission? Where is he now?"

Rebekah swallowed. She could hardly form words about the brutal man who was a blood relative of these sweet girls, and apparently a much different kind of man when he was inside Los Abrigos.

There was no easy way to break the news. "Pinto did kill a lawman in Hagan. He was hanged for it. I'm sorry."

Antonia covered her mouth, tears welling in her eyes. Her tears spilled out and she jumped up from her loom and ran inside the casita. Carmelita sat stock-still, staring at Rebekah, challenging her for the entire truth. She seemed to find it and her eyes dropped, her hands still on the loom.

Rebekah swallowed. "I'm so sorry."

And she truly was. Sorry for the life these girls were raised in. Their grandfather, Gabino Fuentes, was right to grieve not leaving the valley long ago.

They sat there quietly, so the echoes of distant gunfire were clear. Rebekah quickly stood, dropping the ball of yarn, and staring toward the only road leading into the valley. She always sat where she could see it—studying every rock, every dip and curve, every piece of it for when the time came for her escape.

Now a billow of dust rose from the top of the road. A wagon appeared, escorted by three men on horseback and a fourth on the springboard seat. They were shooting in the air and whipping the team as they charged down the hill. Two of the escorts were Sancho and Edgardo Guerra.

The villagers dropped their work and ran to meet the wagon heavily laden with supplies. From the distance of where she stood at the Grande Colina, Rebekah could tell something was being dragged behind the wagon that had probably popped out of the back of it, like the pot that broke loose from the side and fell unheeded.

Rebekah followed Carmelita and other hacienda servants who rushed down the slope and to the center of the village where the wagon was brought to a stop.

One of the horses halted Rebekah in her tracks. He was a magnificent large gray, one very familiar. But it would be impossible for him to be there, in a harness, pulling a wagon into Los Abrigos.

With the dust settling and the mob of villagers converging on the wagon, Rebekah glanced to where the horsemen were nudging close to the item that had fallen out of the wagon and dragged by ropes.

To her horror, she saw the item was a man.

CHAPTER 12

Two shots fired in the air stilled everyone. Rebekah glanced over to Sancho and Edgardo, still seated on their horses. Edgardo holstered his pistol and Sancho sat tall in his saddle, scanning the people with his controlled smile.

"As promised, here are the supplies to begin replenishing the village," he said. "We will soon disperse the supplies. But first, we must deal with a threat to our security."

His gaze fell on the bloodied body behind the wagon. The injured man moved one leg with a moan.

Rebekah's instinct was to rush to him, examine his cuts and scrapes, and check for signs of internal bleeding. But she was frozen in the presence of Sancho. For the moment, he was ignoring her and that felt terribly important.

Sancho turned in the saddle to watch his grandmother, also on horseback, coming down from Grande Colina. Bedecked in jewels and seated like a queen on her throne, Abuelita Guerra rode sidesaddle with her chin raised as she approached the gathering.

The people moved aside and she took her place in the center of them. She stared at the crumpled body behind the wagon.

"Bring this man to the arbor," she commanded.

Rebekah noticed several people looking at the wagon with longing as two men cut the rope loose from the wagon. They lifted the injured man and followed Abuelita Guerra toward an arbor near the road.

The man's head lulled to one side, showing a short white scar on his jaw. Rebekah saw his eyes flicker. He was alive.

As the people slowly moved away from the wagon, Rebekah hesitated, wanting to see if she could sneak something off the wagon that could help with her escape. But from the corner of her eye, she saw Edgardo watching her.

She headed for the arbor, noticing Gabino Fuentes shuffling forward in front of her. He glanced over his shoulder and met Rebekah's eyes. His grave eyes conveyed a message she understood. What was coming would not be good.

The people crowded in the arbor, finding seats on the rows of benches. Rebekah had taken note of this arbor because of its proximity to the road. She had wondered if she could hide supplies among the benches so they were ready for her escape. It was open on all four sides with a thatched roof. A table sat at one end of it, facing the rows of backless wood benches. She thought it was for religious services, but she hadn't seen it used. Until now.

Rebekah slipped onto a bare spot on a bench at the very end of the arbor, next to Carmelita and Antonia. Their father, Martín, sat stone faced on the other side of the girls. His arm was still in a sling, his hand in a clean bandage.

Rebekah wished she'd been called on to take over treatment for his wound, something to show she was indeed a medical doctor and worth keeping alive.

Abuelita Guerra moved around behind a table at the head of the arbor. She pressed her fingertips on it as she faced her subjects and nodded at one of the men.

He went to a nearby well and retrieved a bucketful of water. He dumped the water on the man's face as he lay in the dirt. The man came alive, spitting water and sucking in a deep breath. The two men pulled him to his feet, holding him upright.

From behind, Rebekah could see how limp he was. How helpless. Maybe she could get her medical bag and treat him after the Guerras were finished with him. If he was still alive.

How could she save him? Who was he? A potential ally for her or a rogue trader who accidentally found himself on Sancho Guerra's bad side?

Abuelita Guerra took a seat behind the table, still in Rebekah's view where she sat to the back and left of the arbor. The shade didn't fully cover her, bringing to mind the terrible ride through the desert. She was sweating and the sun burned one side of her face as she waited to discover the man's fate; and if it was tied to her own.

Abuelita Guerra addressed Edgardo. "Who is this man?"

Edgardo, who stood beside his father by their grandmother, took a step forward and spoke for all to hear. "He claims he will sell us supplies and weapons, that he knows one of our men here. He was captured by the first line of guards."

Abuelita Guerra's gaze swept the faces of the crowd. "Does anyone know this man?"

A man to Rebekah's far right stood, holding his sombrero by the rim, sweat dripping down his forehead. "I know him, Señora Guerra. He is from Golden, and claimed knowledge of Los Abrigos and wanted to be a supplier. I told him I would consider presenting his offer to Señor Guerra, but not to come to the valley until he was given permission."

Another man stood. "Señora Guerra, the Mexican army wants very much to invade our valley. This man is likely a spy sent to see our weaknesses."

Edgardo took another step forward, clenching his holstered double pistols. "We have no weaknesses."

There was complete silence under the arbor. Everyone knew the truth yet no one dared speak it.

Señora Guerra slowly rose from her seat. She stood there and made eye contact with every person under the arbor. When she came to Rebekah, Rebekah did her best to maintain a solid gaze in return. The woman lingered on her longer than the others and Rebekah felt something within her crack.

Abuelita Guerra looked back to the trader who was draped limp between the two men. It seemed everyone was on the edge of their bench, awaiting the verdict.

Abuelita Guerra, her movements effortless despite her age, took a step to the side and turned toward Edgardo.

"Give me a pistol."

He stared down at her, a good foot and a half taller than the petite old woman. He hesitated, uncertain, and she snapped her fingers in his face. He quickly withdrew his left pistol and handed it to her, butt first.

Abuelita Guerra took it and came around to the front of the table. She waved at the two men and they dropped the trader to his knees and stepped back. Several people scrambled from the center aisle, out of the line of fire.

Rebekah wanted to jump up and scream.

The man looked up at Abuelita Guerra, meeting her steady gaze. She cocked the pistol, took aim, and fired.

People gasped as the man's body jerked to the side. Rebekah could see the bullet had hit him in the left forearm. She covered her mouth with both hands. Did Abuelita Guerra intend to shoot him one limb at a time?

The man managed to stay upright on his knees, his arm dangling, blood streaming down it and to the ground.

Abuelita Guerra lowered the smoking pistol and raised her gaze to look directly at Rebekah.

"Doc Beck, as you are called across the border, it is time to exhibit your medical skills. Treat this man."

Rebekah pressed her hands tighter against the scream in her

throat. She desperately wanted out of this place, away from these people and their ways.

God, please help me.

Abuelita Guerra went back around the table, handing Edgardo's gun back to him and saying something. He turned with a frown and left the arbor.

Abuelita Guerra took her seat again and glanced over at where Rebekah hadn't moved. The woman looked up at Sancho.

Sancho, with his calm, killer smile, came toward Rebekah. She didn't flinch when he stopped at her side and offered his hand.

"Señorita Rebekah, my grandmother has given you an order. You will obey."

The wounded trader glanced back at the corner, meeting Rebekah's gaze. He was a middle-aged Mexican man with years of experience in his eyes. She felt a sense of decency and honesty about him.

Rebekah suspected the village accuser was right. This man was a spy for the Mexican army. If she could find a way to save him, they could work together on an escape.

Rebekah rose slowly from the bench, letting her hands slide away from her mouth. Her father taught her there were moments to wisely give in and there were moments to stand in true courage. Rebekah knew this moment was both.

She sidestepped Sancho and skirted the cluster of benches to reach the aisle that ran in front of the judgement table. She was aware of everyone in the village watching her.

Edgardo returned, carrying her medical bag. He shoved it into her arms with a look of anger hotter than the noonday sun.

But Rebekah cradled the bag, feeling as though she'd been reunited with a long-lost friend.

She glanced around and spotted the two men who dragged the trader to the arbor. "Please take him to Señor Gabino Fuentes' home. I will treat him there."

Behind her, Abuelita Guerra's steely voice cut through her. "You will treat him here where we can observe."

Rebekah glanced at her sharply, her nature as a physician bolstering her courage. "I cannot treat a patient in the middle of a dirt floor."

Abuelita Guerra lifted her chin and Rebekah knew she would not accept being challenged. Rebekah wondered if this was the place where she would be executed.

A high-pitched voice came from the back of the arbor. "Señorita Rebekah, you can do it." It was Antonia. "We will help."

Rebekah glanced back to see the younger Fuentes sister on her feet and tugging on her sister's arm. Carmelita was pale, the whites of her eyes showing as Antonia pulled her to her feet.

Rebekah could scarcely believe Antonia's bravery, willing to step in even after the news Rebekah shared about the law and the sisters' uncle Pinto.

The girls came arm in arm to stand behind the kneeling trader. Antonia looked at Rebekah, her eyes pleading with Rebekah not to get herself killed.

Antonia's courage both inspired and frightened Rebekah. If she failed, the sisters would suffer too.

Rebekah swallowed and motioned to the empty bench in front of Abuelita Guerra's table. "Let's get him laying down here, out of the dust."

One hand clutching the handle of her medical bag, Rebekah helped the trader on one side while the sisters lifted him. Together, they were able to get him stretched out on the narrow bench.

Antonia knelt under his wounded arm and held it up with her hands. Rebekah took a deep breath and joined her on the ground, opening her bag. She ran her fingers over the instruments at the top, the coolness of them calming her. She would start with the bullet wound and then treat his injuries from being dragged behind the wagon.

This was work she'd trained to do. She could do it even at Los Abrigos.

Rebekah spoke to Carmelita. "*Agua.*"

Carmelita rose and went to fetch the bucket from the well. Rebekah's eyes followed her long enough to catch the look exchanged between her and Edgardo. It was a tragic sight. Edgardo was on the verge of becoming irredeemable.

As Rebekah tore away the bloody sleeve, the trader rolled his head toward Antonia and asked in English, "What is your name, child?"

Antonia looked at Rebekah, startled. Why had the man spoken English, a language Antonia had never heard?

Rebekah grew up in a home of three languages. But this was a blessed relief to hear.

Rebekah started to translate for Antonia, but the man spoke again, this time to Rebekah. His words were so low, she could barely understand them.

"Doctor, we are here to get you out. Be ready."

Rebekah froze, staring into his soft brown eyes that begged her to trust him. She did. She had to. But who sent him? What did he mean by "we"? Was the Mexican army about to attack?

Carmelita came back with a bucket and set it next to Rebekah. She went to work, ignoring how she and her patient—her would-be rescuer—were on display before the whole village, under the scrutiny of Abuelita Guerra.

Rebekah labored over the trader, suturing his arm wound and treating the tears in his flesh from being dragged. She discovered two broken ribs and wrapped his midsection tightly in a bandage.

When Rebekah wiped the sweat from her forehead, she used the opportunity to look around her. The villagers watched from the benches or stood at the edge of the arbor, solemn. She kept her back to Abuelita Guerra and the judgment table. She already knew what that woman and her family's intentions were. Any hope Rebekah and the trader had of escaping would come from the people.

Rebekah finished her work with wiping the trader's bruised face with a damp cloth.

He smiled up at her, weak, and said, *"Gracias."*

"De nada."

Rebekah cleaned her instruments and replaced them in her bag while the sisters stayed on each side of the man, partially supporting him on the narrow bench.

Rebekah flicked her gaze up to Abuelita Guerra, wondering if she was going to come close and inspect Rebekah's work. The woman stood from the table and nodded at Rebekah as though they were in a classroom of medical students.

"Doctor Rebekah, you know your work well." Abuelita Guerra announced it like she was giving a commencement speech. "You will be a valuable asset to our community."

Rebekah reached for her bag as she stood, holding it close to her side, hiding it with her skirt. She hoped to keep it close from now on. The weight told her it no longer held her pepperbox pistol, but there were other useful items in it for her escape.

Rebekah motioned to the trader. "I would like to have him moved to the Fuentes' quarters where I can monitor his condition. He is severely injured."

Abuelita Guerra pressed her fingertips against the table again. "That will not be necessary. Edgardo, kill him."

Rebekah lost her breath and the medical bag landed in the dirt beside her with a thump. The Fuentes sisters gasped, and Antonia began to cry.

Edgardo glanced at his grandmother and his father. The hesitation was there, but gone in a flash. He wouldn't disappoint them. He moved from behind the judgement table, drawing one of his pistols.

Rebekah couldn't think, only do. She stepped in front of Edgardo, her arms spread wide to shield the sisters and the trader.

Edgardo cocked the pistol.

Rebekah wasn't aware of Sancho's presence until he grabbed her by the wrist and yanked her away. She gasped and swung around to kick him, but he held her tight.

The report of a gunshot and screams echoed behind her.

CHAPTER 13

The night air cooled Rebekah's cheeks as she stepped out onto the Grande Colina terrace from the hacienda. She moved toward the stone ramp that led from the terrace to the yard below.

She touched the cool stone railing of the terrace, her heart desperate for something that would not harm her or her heart. Sitting through a late-evening dinner with all three Guerras was almost more than she could bear.

After Edgardo shot the trader point blank, Rebekah vaguely recalled old Gabino Fuentes' sad eyes. Those eyes haunted her now as she looked out beyond the adobe homes and the valley itself to the road.

She contemplated walking down the stone terrace ramp, down the hill, through the adobe casitas and corrals, and straight up that road to freedom.

Was living really better than dying in this place?

A man gave his life trying to free Rebekah. She didn't deserve that. She could only accept his gift and try to make it out alive if the Mexican army did attack.

Footsteps on the stone floor of the terrace jolted Rebekah and she glanced back to see Edgardo exiting the front double doors. He barely looked her way as he went down the steps on the other side. He was headed toward the servants' quarters. Specifically, toward the Fuentes sisters'.

Rebekah wanted to run after him, tackle him, stop him from doing any more harm. But she was helpless as a lamb lost in the mountains, far from the protection of a shepherd. She had been that way a long time, but it never felt like this.

She moved to the darkest corner of the terrace, away from light streaming through the front windows.

The stars were a perfect dome above her, shining of magnificence she couldn't comprehend. She whispered a prayer in her Omaha tongue, the words belonging to her father.

Lord, let me do what is right and fight what is wrong. My soul is in Your care. Amen.

It was the fullest prayer Rebekah had prayed in years. Perhaps the Shepherd would come to her. Her father believed that.

Rebekah's eyes roamed to the road again, visible by the torches that lit it. How could she possibly escape up it?

Something below the road caught her eye, a long shadow near the horse corral. As she studied the shadow, the form of a man developed then darted behind the casita of the family Rebekah had seen on her first day of wandering the village.

There, the man appeared again, easing around the corner of the home. The children's puppy bounded out of a box in the yard and the man squatted to scratch the puppy behind the ears. The animal didn't make a sound, like this was someone it knew. Or at least, now trusted.

As the man rose, his shoulders dipped left and then right.

There was something incredibly familiar about the movement. Rebekah crossed her arms and hugged herself tight, willing her eyes to clear and identify or disregard the shadowy figure. Before she could do either, the man disappeared in the mesquite trees and brush leading up to the Grande Colina Hacienda.

Rebekah stared at the brush for several seconds, willing the man to reappear. He didn't.

She closed her eyes and drew in a shaky breath. She was so desperate for hope, but there was no one in this valley except whomever Abuelita Guerra allowed. And that was no one who wanted to help Rebekah.

Rebekah opened her eyes and saw one of the yucca scrubs near the terrace wall shaking as though someone just disturbed it. A white flower flew through the air from behind her and landed at her feet.

A voice spoke, close and deep. "Becka."

She jerked her rigid body to face right, staring at the manicured trees that stood sentry close to the wall of the hacienda. She stared at the trees until a man materialized out of them.

He was tall, with a battered sombrero pulled low to hide his face. But she didn't need to see his features to recognize the voice that sounded like a deep well. A serape covered his shoulders, but they were as broad and strong under the blanket as they had been under the gold officer bars of a U.S. Cavalry uniform so many years ago.

Here stood Rebekah's reason for not wanting to return to Wyoming. Yet she was indescribably relieved.

By some miracle, he was actually there. How could that be?

The man put his hands on the rail and vaulted the low stone wall to stand within a few feet of her.

Rebekah breathed, "Lee. Lee Stafford, what in heaven's name are you doing here?"

He swiped off the sombrero, revealing his dark brown hair, unkempt to match his disguise. His light smile pierced her soul.

"Just rounding up a lost steer, ma'am."

Rebekah swallowed, hard. The timbre of his voice took her back, not to McKinnon Ranch, but to the days of her youth on the Omaha Reservation. His voice hadn't been as deep then, nor had dignified white flecks in his hair touched his ears. But there was a sense of belonging in that voice. She belonged with it, back in Wyoming, the place she had resisted for too long.

Lee Stafford—or Laramie Jones as he was known to the rest of the world—broke into her memories to create a new one.

"I'm here to take you home, Becka."

Home. Was there really a chance of getting back there?

She looked up at him, seeing his face pinched.

"The trader's dead, isn't he?" he asked. "Fernando Contrera?"

Rebekah wanted to weep at the look of grief in his eyes. She could only nod.

Laramie did, too, and glanced at the light coming from the Grande Colina Hacienda. He spoke to her while keeping watch. "Contrera was with the Rurales. He got me in here with a false bottom in his wagon. Planned to leave the same way, but we'll have to scale the valley wall like billy goats. You'll need to get some trousers and—"

His instructions were disrupted by a wail coming from the direction of the servants' quarters.

Rebekah froze in the shadow of the trees while Laramie vaulted back over the stone rail. He reached for her but Rebekah took several steps away. Laramie needed to hide until they could safely escape. Being with him now would only put him in danger.

The double front doors opened, spilling more light onto the terrace. But the light was cut in half by Sancho stepping out. His grandmother came out beside him, her regal poise undeterred by another desperate wail.

Edgardo climbed the side steps of the terrace, his hand twisted in the worn serape of old Gabino Fuentes, pulling him along. Carmelita and Antonia followed, both crying as Carmelita held her little sister close.

Edgardo pushed the old man down to his knees before Sancho and Abuelita Guerra.

Antonia spotted Rebekah. She tore from her sister's hold and ran over. She grabbed Rebekah by the arms, her breath coming in great gasps.

"Please, Señorita Rebekah, help my grandfather! They will kill him for what he said."

CHAPTER 14

Rebekah had never felt so utterly helpless as she did in that moment. Edgardo's eyes blazed as he spoke to his grandmother.

"I would have shot this old man as soon as the words left his mouth, but I wanted you to spit in his face first, say what a liar he is."

Sancho hooked one thumb behind the hammer of his six gun. How quickly he had strapped it back on after the dinner table, and Edgardo as well.

Sancho's voice sounded strained when he asked, "What is this lie he has told, my son?"

Edgardo stared at his grandmother. "He says...I cannot even speak it."

Old Gabino put his hands on his knees and raised his head to look at Abuelita Guerra. "I spoke the truth." His voice quivered then strengthened. "I spoke the truth to him so that he may know the kind of man he will become when he listens to you—the kind of man his father became."

Gabino paused and there was a deadly silence before he finished with, "I told of how you killed Edgardo's mother."

Rebekah slipped both arms around Antonia's waist, holding her tight as the girl began to weep again.

Edgardo grabbed the back of the man's neck and shoved him hard to the floor. The old man's hands went out to catch himself, but he failed, and his face smacked into the stone floor.

Edgardo looked to his grandmother. "Spit on him and then I will kill him."

Sancho shifted his feet and his eyes came up to meet Rebekah's. He gave her his odd little smile and it chilled her like never before. He glanced down at his son.

"Abuelita warned me not to marry your mother; that she was an outsider and would not accept our ways. You must understand, my son—she could have destroyed our village."

The deadly silence stretched again. Edgardo, his face pale, slowly raised, releasing the old man's neck.

His grandmother, her chin high, said, "Your grandfather was of the same sort, turning the people against me. That was why Sancho hated him. As for your mother...I was forced to poison her slowly, the same as she was poisoning our people against me. You would not have had your home, your very life ways, had I not done this."

Edgardo took a step back, his jaw slack. Rebekah stroked Antonia's hair, unable to breathe in the thickness of the air on the terrace. Carmelita stood with her hands over her mouth as though stifling a scream that would echo all the way up the road to freedom.

Edgardo shook his head. "No." His voice sounded like a strangled animal. He shouted, "No! Those weeks she was ill, when I stayed at her bedside, when she was crying out for a priest or a nun to come and pray for her. That was not caused by you."

Abuelita Guerra stepped further onto the terrace, blocking more light from behind her, shadowing her grandson's face.

"I must be obeyed without question or our society can no longer exist," she spat. "This is something your father understands and it is something you now will come to understand. I have taken your desires into careful consideration and made my decision."

Abuelita Guerra turned sharply, facing Rebekah. She spoke to Edgardo. "You will kill this lady doctor before she poisons our people anymore. Do it now!"

Antonia screamed into Rebekah's shoulder where her face was pressed tight. Rebekah instinctively loosened her grip on the girl as Edgardo slowly turned toward them, his fingers wrapping around the butt of his pistol.

Carmelita screamed, "Edgardo, no!"

Rebekah stared into his eyes, shadowed by the lack of light, and drowning in the darkness of this place.

Rebekah took Antonia by the shoulders and forced her away, out of the line of fire. She knew what Edgardo would do and she wanted to be ready for her next move. Only God knew what that was.

Where was Laramie?

Edgardo's grip on his holstered pistol tightened until his arm shook. The shaking made its way to his head and the rest of his body until he was shaking uncontrollably.

He let out a strangled cry and dropped to one knee, burying his face in his arm. He released the grip on his pistol and his hand dangled loose.

Abuelita Guerra clenched her jaw and took a step back to nod at Sancho.

Sancho let out a heavy sigh as he spoke to Edgardo. "You disappoint me, my son. I thought you had finally become a man, but I see you never will."

Sancho's hand dropped to his gun. As Carmelita screamed again, Gabino pushed up to his hands and knees, a stream of blood running from his nose. He staggered forward, partly on his feet, and grabbed Sancho's gun arm with both hands. The rage in

Sancho's eyes was one Rebekah recognized. She only had a few seconds.

She hooked Antonia around the waist and dragged her to the side of the terrace. She looked back in time to see Sancho whack the old man away and raise his pistol.

Edgardo jumped to his feet, shouting, "No, Papá!"

He drew his gun and Sancho turned instinctively toward him. His gun went off. The bullet struck Edgardo in the gut, freezing the young man on his feet. Then he collapsed.

Sancho's smoking barrel turned toward where Rebekah had shoved Antonia close to the rail of the terrace. She hovered over the girl.

Another shot echoed over the stone, and Rebekah gripped Antonia's shoulder hard.

Sancho took one step forward and then another before crumbling at the feet of Gabino Fuentes. But it wasn't the old man who shot Sancho Guerra.

Rebekah twisted to where she was on her hands and knees, facing the scene.

Laramie Jones, six-gun smoking, leaped over the wall and onto the terrace.

Abuelita Guerra stared at the bodies of her grandsons. Her chin went higher, higher, higher. She gripped the bodice of her dress and dropped to her knees then slumped down face first onto the terrace.

Gabino Fuentes went to pry Sancho's gun from his limp hand. Carmelita ran to Edgardo. Rebekah, helped by Antonia, got to her feet and went to Abuelita Guerra. She knelt by the woman's quivering form, turned her over, and into her arms.

Abuelita Guerra's eyes were red like a demon from the Bible. Her hand came up, claw-like, from her chest and reached for Rebekah's throat. Abuelita Guerra clamped on, but there was no strength to squeeze.

Rebekah slowly reached up and took the woman's wrist,

pulling her hand away. She said quietly to Antonia, who had followed her, "She is having a heart attack. Go fetch my medical bag please."

Her words faded at the end to match Abuelita Guerra's fading heartbeat. It faded away into the stillness.

❧

THE GUNSHOTS AWOKE the entire village. As Rebekah lowered Abuelita Guerra to the cold floor of the terrace, she was aware of the people rushing up the hill to the Grande Colina Hacienda.

Laramie knelt by Rebekah's side, gripping her forearm. "Time for us to git, Becka. We'll make a run for the road on Slate. He was part of Contrera's wagon team."

The hot metal of his gun barrel was near her bare hand—the gun that killed Sancho Guerra and freed her at last.

As she looked around at the scene on the terrace with Gabino Fuentes embracing his two granddaughters, she knew she was not the only one free.

Rebekah let Laramie help her to her feet, but she stayed rooted in place when he tried to pull her away. "Wait, Lee," she whispered. "We'll be shot if we run, but I don't think we'll need to."

First onto the terrace was Martín Fuentes, his un-bandaged hand showing no injury, only a scar. He halted and stared in shock at the three bodies spread before him. The other villagers came up behind him and made a solemn line from one end of the terrace to the other. They were in disbelief.

No one cried.

Old Gabino turned to his son. They looked at one another a good long while in the silence before Martín finally turned and addressed his fellow villagers.

"We were fearful of this time coming. We were fearful of it not. I am the greatest coward among you." He raised his scarred hand. "I did this. I shot my own hand to keep from going out on that long ride with Sancho. I am filled with that much fear. But no more!" His voice boomed. "For too long, the Guerras have lorded over our lives with fear and violence. It is time for us to live!"

Families bunched close together, holding on to one another, and the tears finally came. Whether in grief for the poor lives they had lived or for the lives they could now live, Rebekah couldn't judge.

Old Gabino shuffled toward her, supported by his granddaughters. He reached out to pat Rebekah's cheek. "We will send messengers out to the guards that you and your friend are to leave in peace. You have nothing more to fear in this valley, Señorita Rebekah."

Martín strode over to them. He quickly kissed his daughters on the cheeks, then turned them toward Rebekah.

"Señorita, you know many of us will be arrested by the army soon. These two children have never committed a crime, but will become outcasts in their own country and destitute. Please, Señorita, will you take my daughters from here with you? Take them and show them there is a world beyond these walls."

Antonia cried out and wrapped her arms around her father's neck. Old Gabino reached up to grip his son's shoulder in a gesture of pride. A tear made its way down the ravines of his face.

Carmelita looked stunned. She glanced over to where one of the village men was covering Edgardo's body with a blanket.

She reached out and touched her sister's arm. "Kiss your grandfather and your father goodbye. We will do as he says."

Within half an hour, Rebekah was seated in Fernando Contrera's wagon, on the springboard bench next to Laramie. The Fuentes sisters were in the wagon bed with their few possessions and enough supplies to see them all to the border.

Laramie's big gray horse, Slate, was hitched to the wagon with

Contrera's horse. Rebekah should have recognized Slate right away when she saw him earlier.

Laramie shook the reins and the team took off. He aimed them up the road to freedom.

Rebekah gripped the wagon bench, feeling as though she'd been underwater for so long she had nearly drowned and now, there was the surface, rushing closer and closer to meet her.

There were no guards at the top of the hill. All of Sancho's bandits had fled the valley, knowing the Mexican army was coming and the villagers would let them in.

The wagon suddenly reached the top, and the ground leveled. Rebekah sucked in a deep breath, finally above the surface of the water. She drew in another breath and another. She couldn't stop.

Laramie slowed the horses and held the reins in his left hand while he put his other arm around her shoulders. "It's all right, Becka. I'll have you home soon."

Home. How sweet and foreign that word was.

CHAPTER 15

They stopped off at the town of Golden to pick up Just Jimmy from jail there. After a fierce hug for Rebekah, he didn't stop talking for two hours as he stood behind the bench, alternating between telling Rebekah about his short adventure in trying to rescue her, to attempting to engage the Fuentes sisters in conversation through his broken Spanish. At least his Spanish had improved over the past few weeks in the jail where he'd had all the drunks and town disruptors for cell mates.

Carmelita never said a word, but Rebekah glanced back a few times to see Antonia smiling and trying to talk to the young white man, the first she'd ever met.

They were escorted to the border by the Rurales and greeted on the other side by Marshal Lopez and Sheriff Thad Biggins, who took them on to Zapata.

There, Rebekah said a tearful goodbye to the Fuentes sisters who had taken such fine care of her. She left them in the tender hands of Bernadette Peterson, knowing the woman was the most capable of introducing them to the outside world.

Antonia begged to go on with Rebekah, and Rebekah promised to come back and see the sisters someday. Or perhaps they could come visit where Rebekah was going. But this was not the right time. The sisters needed to get acclimated in a familiar landscape, not the lush green pastures and valleys of Wyoming.

When they left the wagon at the Zapata livery stables, Rebekah touched the bench in thankfulness for the man who had given his life to save her.

Greater love hath no man than this, that a man lay down his life for his friends.

She had experienced yet another one of her father's favorite scripture verses. Fernando Contrera had given his life for her; Laramie Jones and Just Jimmy had been willing to. Because of them, she was alive.

In the same hotel room she stayed in after her first ordeal with Sancho Guerra at the mission, Rebekah tossed and turned, unable to sleep. Dawn was a relief, along with boarding the train bound for Wyoming—at last.

Laramie sat on the bench beside her, Jimmy across from them. Her medical bag, with the pepperbox gun she recovered from Sancho's gun case in the hacienda, rested between her feet. It was comforting to keep it close.

Jimmy seemed to have slept well in the room he shared with Laramie, but there were still dark circles under his eyes.

He leaned forward, propping his elbows on his knees. "I sure was worried about you, Miss Rebekah," he said quietly. "Never prayed so much in my life. Even my cellmate prayed for you, and he didn't even believe in God, I don't think." He looked to Laramie. "What was that he said when you got me out of there? I can do better with Spanish now, but couldn't make out what he said."

Laramie smiled. "He said something about living more like you from now on."

Jimmy cocked his head. "I wasn't really living much. I was just in jail, praying and wishing I could read this." He reached into his jacket pocket and pulled out his New Testament.

Rebekah stared at it. "There are many stories in there of men who lived the best parts of their lives in prisons and lion's dens, praying."

She shook herself and quickly added, "We will teach you to read, Jimmy. And we are going to have the biggest and best birthday celebration for you that the McKinnon Ranch has ever seen."

Jimmy smiled. "I don't reckon that's nearly as important to me now, Miss Rebekah, but I know what date I want for keeps—the day you got set free from that bandit hole, whatever date that was. Would you write it in my Bible for me?"

Jimmy held it out to her and Laramie handed her a pencil from his vest pocket. Rebekah took the items and opened the worn book. She wished—almost expected—for Jimmy's full name to be in there, and the real record of his birth. But the records in the front were blank.

She wrote "Just Jimmy" and added the date of her freedom. Her hands shook as she handed the pencil back to Laramie and the book to Jimmy.

Jimmy took it, his eyes suddenly filled with tears. "Thank you, Miss Rebekah. I sure am sorry I wasn't any help in getting you out."

Rebekah blinked, surprised her own tears still hadn't come. "I think, maybe, Jimmy, that you did help more than any of us will ever know."

She gave him the best smile she could. "And it's all right. Lee was there."

Jimmy raised an eyebrow and glanced around, looking to see if there was someone else with them. "Lee?"

Laramie Jones tugged on his vest as if to straighten it. Rebekah looked up at him apologetically, but he grinned and spoke to Jimmy.

"Me and Miss Rebekah have known one another a good spell, Jimmy. She's the only one these days who calls me Lee. I'd appreciate it if you would remember that.”

Jimmy returned the grin. “Sure, I know how that is. But I’m reckoning you’re a mighty good man, being one of Doc Beck’s old friends.”

❧

WHEN THE TRAIN pulled into Centennial Ridge, Wyoming, Rebekah was half asleep. Yet she was conscious of what she was about to face, the world she was going to re-enter. She just wanted to get to her final destination as soon as possible.

There were familiar faces at the depot, including Marshal Dave Thorp and top hands from the ranch like Steve Bowers. All who had big grins for her. There were familiar town faces too, but Rebekah gratefully let Laramie hand her into a covered buggy from the McKinnon Ranch while Steve held the reins.

Laramie and Steve took the front bench, while she settled in the back with Jimmy, medical bag on the seat between them. Now that they were past the initial relief of the ordeal coming to an end, Jimmy could hardly contain his excitement. He gripped the buggy frame and scanned the verdant foothills of the Medicine Bow Mountains in summertime.

“You reckon Doctor McKinnon will really give me a job on his ranch?” he asked.

Rebekah patted his hand. “I’ll put in a good word with the foreman.”

“Who’s the foreman?”

Rebekah nodded toward Laramie’s back. Jimmy gaped at her and Rebekah chuckled. It wasn’t a full laugh, but a genuine one. It relieved some of the tension in her body. Yet not all.

The ride was quiet and long, but they finally rolled up the graveled road leading to the two-story mansion Rebekah had known since childhood. The white columns supporting the wide front porch were due for a new coat of paint and the house was weather worn—but she had never seen a more beautiful sight.

Rebekah grabbed the buggy frame, blood pulsing through her temples. She didn't know why she was both anxious and thrilled.

Before Laramie pulled the horses to a complete stop, Rebekah held her skirt close and sprang from the buggy. She landed on the walkway, giving no backward glance to her medical bag. She didn't need it for that moment.

An aging gentleman with a soft, dignified expression stood on the porch. He unhooked his thumbs from his vest pockets and came down the steps as though he were twenty years younger than his age.

For all her pent up energy of finally being there, Rebekah couldn't move. She stood by the buggy, arms limp at her sides.

Doctor Robert T. McKinnon came to a halt before her, his eyes brimming with tears. He engulfed her in a hug like they had never shared before.

His strength filled Rebekah's arms and she raised them to return the embrace, laying her head against his shoulder. She inhaled the scents of woodsmoke and earth on his leather vest. It brought out memories of the Omaha Reservation, and her parents, and school, and a whole lifetime.

She closed her eyes and whispered into his vest, "I'm home, Uncle Robert."

Dearest reader,

Thank you for reading *Desert Captive (Doc Beck Westerns Book 4)*. I truly hope it entertained and delighted you!

If you fell in love with the main characters, Rebekah, aka "Doc Beck," and Jimmy, you'll be excited to know there are more books to come!

Meanwhile, I'd be thrilled if you took a moment to write your thoughts in the form of a review for *Desert Captive* and post it on your favorite retail outlet and Goodreads. You'll help other readers find this series.

To discover more of my books, free short stories, and to generally stay in touch with me, I invite you to join my VIP reader newsletter. You'll receive a free copy of *The Executions*, book one in my historical fiction *Choctaw Tribune* series. Please join me here.

Speaking of history, the character of Doc Beck was inspired by Dr. Susan La Flesche (Omaha), who is hailed as the first American Indian to earn a medical degree. In continued research, my mother found Dr. Isabel Cobb (Cherokee), the first woman physician in Indian Territory, in very nearly the same years as Dr. La Flesche.

Lastly, if you're not familiar with my heritage books based on my Choctaw history and culture, you can check them out on my website.

Questions? Send them my way: me@sarahelisabethwrites.com

—Sarah Elisabeth Sawyer
Historical Fiction and Western author
Tribal member of the Choctaw Nation of Oklahoma

CANYON WAR (DOC BECK WESTERNS BOOK 1)

Traveling the West as a female physician, 34-year-old Doctor Rebekah LaRoche is no stranger to trouble. But on her way to New Mexico Territory, an unexpected stay in Amarillo, Texas, leads to confrontation with the Baxter clan – four brothers bred for trouble – and finds Rebekah in deep trouble.

Cattle rancher Clem Baxter's private war over grazing rights in the Palo Duro Canyon turns disastrous, and when the dust settles, one of the Baxter brothers is hurt bad. Clem sends for a doctor, not a woman, but that's what he gets when Rebekah, known as "Doc Beck," arrives at the ranch.

Now held at Clem's ranch against her will, Rebekah must plot to flee through the night with her young friend into the dangers and beauty of the Palo Duro Canyon.

Of Omaha Indian and French descent, Rebekah has always relied on her wits to get her out of any situation. But does that include facing down men willing to die—and kill—for a wild piece of land just as dangerous as any bullet?

Canyon War is available on multiple retailer sites.

◆ ◆ ◆

MISSION BANDITS (DOC BECK WESTERNS BOOK 2)

The Mexican army, a town marshal, and the Sancho Guerra gang are facing off when Doctor Rebekah LaRoche and her new friend, Jimmy, arrive in Zapata, New Mexico Territory. The bandits are holding hostages at Hope Academy, a school for girls located in an old mission outside of town, and Rebekah feels compelled to act—she was sent to the school to modernize the infirmary, not see the innocent occupants murdered.

The notorious and charismatic bandit, Sancho Guerra, led his band of men on a pillaging spree from Mexico to the mission and has proven his indifference to killing, prepared for any tricks the army or the Zapata town marshal throw at him.

But he isn't prepared for Rebekah, and now the Mexican army colonel wants her to do something terrifying—enter the mission and help with the capture of the deadliest men in the territory.

Mission Bandits is available on multiple retailer sites.

♦♦♦

GRAVE ROBBERS (DOC BECK WESTERNS BOOK 3)

"You swing just as high for killing one as you do three."

Called on to perform an autopsy for a murder case, Doctor Rebekah LaRoche and Just Jimmy find themselves as unlikely detectives in a town with too many secrets.

One of the bandits who held the old mission and Rebekah hostage is accused of murdering Ruby Palmer, a young woman who took some of those secrets with her in death. When Rebekah discovers them during the autopsy, she must fight to prove her former captor is innocent. But she soon learns truth isn't something this town welcomes.

There isn't one straight shooter in the lot—the corrupt sheriff, judge, and leading townsmen are ready to lynch the bandit with hardly a trial. The only man Rebekah partly trusts is Deputy Thad Biggins. But what secret is driving him?

With the whole town against her, Rebekah finds herself at a crossroads: Let the bandit guilty of many crimes hang for one he didn't commit; or prove his innocence by robbing Ruby Palmer's grave.

Grave Robbers is available on multiple retailer sites.

◆◆◆

Who would show up for their own execution?

It's 1892, Indian Territory. A war is brewing in the Choctaw Nation as two political parties fight out issues of old and new ways. Caught in the middle is eighteen-year-old Ruth Ann, a Choctaw who doesn't want to see her family killed.

In a small but booming pre-statehood town, her mixed blood family owns a controversial newspaper, the *Choctaw Tribune*. Ruth Ann wants to help spread the word about critical issues but there is danger for a female reporter on all fronts—socially, politically, even physically.

But what is truly worth dying for? This quest leads Ruth Ann and her brother Matthew, the stubborn editor of the fledgling *Choctaw Tribune*, to old Choctaw ways at the farm of a condemned murderer. It also brings them to head on clashes with leading townsmen who want their reports silenced no matter what.

More killings are ahead. Who will survive to know the truth? Will truth survive?

The Executions is available on multiple retailer sites.

TRAITORS (CHOCTAW TRIBUNE SERIES, BOOK 2)

"Someone's going to be king in this territory.
No reason it can't be me. It sure won't be you."

Betrayed.

Someone is tearing at the fabric of the Choctaw Nation while political turmoil, assassinations, and feuds threaten the very sovereignty of the tribe. It stands under the U.S. government's scrutiny.

When heated words turn to hot lead, Ruth Ann Teller—a mixed-blood Choctaw—fears losing her brother who won't settle for anything but the truth. Matthew is determined to use his newspaper, the *Choctaw Tribune*, to uncover the scheme behind Mayor Thaddeus Warren's claim to the townsite of Dickens. Matthew is willing to risk his newspaper—and his life—to uncover a traitor among their Choctaw people.

But when Ruth Ann tries to help, she causes more harm than good—especially after the mayor brings in Lance Fuller, a schoolteacher from

New York. How does this charming yet aloof young man fit into the mayor's scheme?

When attacks against the newspaper strike and bullets fly, a trip to the Chicago World's Fair of 1893 is the answer they need to save the Choctaw Tribune. The trip holds a key to Matthew's investigation.

But Ruth Ann must find the courage to face a journey to the White City —without her brother.

***Traitors* is available on multiple retailer sites.**

◆ ◆ ◆

SHAFT OF TRUTH (CHOCTAW TRIBUNE SERIES, BOOK 3)

"Nothing to it but a stout heart."

On a mission to bring justice to the outlaw gang that murdered his father and brother, Matthew Teller leaves the *Choctaw Tribune* newspaper for his sister to operate and plunges into an unfamiliar world of darkness and danger. Working inside the coal mines of the Choctaw Nation—one of the most dangerous places in the country—he searches for a man who may have the answers to this six-year-old mystery. But after Matthew uncovers an earth-shattering truth that rocks him to his core, he must decide what right is, and what price he is willing to pay for it.

Ruth Ann Teller knows she can handle publishing the *Choctaw Tribune*—until she loses their biggest advertiser. Now, with Matthew miles away and the future of the newspaper resting squarely on her shoulders, Ruth Ann must make a bold move to keep the newspaper afloat in her brother's absence. She sets it on a course for new success or total disaster.

Striking coal miners. Outlaw gangs. An unsolved crime. And a Choctaw family that fights for one another, and for truth.

Shaft of Truth (*Choctaw Tribune* Series, Book 3) is available on multiple retailer sites.

◆◆◆

ANUMPA WARRIOR: CHOCTAW CODE TALKERS OF WORLD WAR I

The day I betrayed Isaac, I vowed never again to speak my native language in front of white men.

When America enters the Great War in 1917, Bertram Robert Dunn and his Choctaw buddies from Armstrong Academy join the army to protect their homes, their families, and their country. Hoping to find redemption for a horrible lie that betrayed his best friend, B.B. heads into the trenches of France—but what he discovers is a duty only his native tongue can fulfill.

War correspondent Matthew Teller is ready to quit until an encounter with a fellow Choctaw sets him on a path to write the untold story of American Indian doughboys. But entrenched stereotypes and prejudices tear at his burning desire to spread truth.

With the Allies building toward the greatest offensive drive of the war, the American Expeditionary Forces face a superior enemy who intercepts their messages and knows their every move. Can the solution come from a people their own government stripped of culture and language?

***Anumpa Warrior* is available on multiple retailer sites.**

◆ ◆ ◆

TOUCH MY TEARS: TALES FROM THE TRAIL OF TEARS

For this collection of short stories, Choctaw authors from five U.S. states came together to present a part of their ancestors' journey, a way to honor those who walked the trail for their future. These stories not only capture a history and a culture, but the spirit, faith, and resilience of the Choctaw people.

Tears of sadness. Tears of joy. Touch and experience them.

Touch My Tears is available on multiple retailer sites.

TUSHPA'S STORY (Touch My Tears Collection)

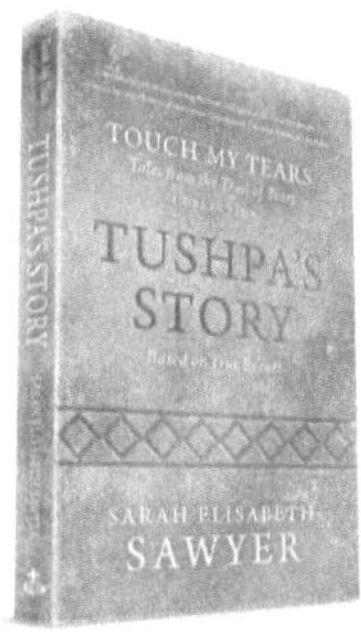

"Protect the book as you do our seed corn. We must have both to survive."

The Treaty of Dancing Rabbit Creek changed everything. The Choctaw Nation could no longer remain in their ancient homelands.

Young Tushpa, his family, and their small band embark on a trail of life and death. More death than life lay ahead.

On their journey to a new homeland, the faith of his father and one book guide Tushpa as he learns what it means to become a man and a leader.

But before long, betrayal from within and without rip at the unity of the band. Can Tushpa help keep his tattered people together? Or will they all be lost to sickness of the mind, body, and spirit on the four hundred mile walk?

A continuation of the anthology *Touch My Tears: Tales from the Trail of Tears*, this story follows an original manuscript written by Tushpa's son, James Culberson.

Tushpa's Story is available on multiple retailer sites.

SARAH ELISABETH SAWYER is a story archaeologist. She digs up shards of past lives, hopes, and truths, and pieces them together for readers today. The Smithsonian's National Museum of the American Indian honored her as a literary artist through their Artist Leadership Program for her work in preserving Choctaw Trail of Tears stories. A tribal member of the Choctaw Nation of Oklahoma, she writes historical fiction from her hometown in Texas, partnering with her mother, Lynda Kay Sawyer, in continued research for future works. Learn more at SarahElisabethWrites.com, Facebook.com/SarahElisabethSawyer